PRAISE FOR THE UNCOOPERATIVE FLYING CARPET

Very well written in concise language and divided into 63 chapters of 2/3 pages each. You can pick it up and read for ten minutes then come back, but you won't—it is too exciting for that. Believable fantasy and behind it all is a sharp sense of humour that even adults will appreciate. A book that demands to be read aloud to children from 8—13 years old.
Bob Docherty, https://bobsbooksnz.wordpress.com/

There is so much to like about this book: the wry humour and sense of fun throughout make the story a joy to read, and I think it would work well as a read-aloud story, as well as one for children to read to themselves. Also, the print version of the book is available for dyslexic readers – a definite plus.
Thebookreviewers.com

I'm a grade 5 teacher and constantly looking out for new novels to read to my extremely creative and imaginative students. I tried this novel because my group have an interested in fantastic adventures and none of us were disappointed. I've begun creating some worksheets and class projects based on the story and characters and my students have really bought into the whole world created by Clark McConnochie. I believe a sequel is in the pipeline and look forward to it eagerly.
Bruce S, Amazon

A children's book which is not only very exciting but which also fosters the concepts of kindness to others and to animals.
Reviewer, Amazon

Highly entertaining and non-stop storyline. Lots of quirky characters, fun twists and even branches out into a few puns - but not too many, so don't be afraid! Should be devoured by the middle-grade readers (with special dyslexia-friendly version available) and was definitely enjoyed by this grown-up kid!
LemurKat, Amazon

A delightful read. Definitely a book I will share with my Grands. Joy **Flynn, Amazon**

Delightful and suspenseful reading! Shows great imagination. Enjoyed reading and had trouble putting down/pausing even though I am an adult!
Pete & Peggy, Amazon

COMING SOON

THE UNCOOPERATIVE FLYING CARPET
SAGA 2 OF THE STRANGE SAGAS
OF SABRINA SUMMERS

THE UNCONTROLLABLE SLINGSHOT
SAGA 3 OF THE STRANGE SAGAS
OF SABRINA SUMMERS

⌒THE⌒
UNCOOPERATIVE
FLYING CARPET
The STRANGE SAGAS of SABRINA SUMMERS

MICHELE CLARK McCONNOCHIE

NEW YORK

LONDON • NASHVILLE • MELBOURNE • VANCOUVER

The Uncooperative Flying Carpet

The Strange Sagas of Sabrina Summers

© 2018 Michele Clark McConnochie

Published in New York, New York, by Morgan James Publishing. Morgan James is a trademark of Morgan James, LLC. www.MorganJamesPublishing.com

ISBN 9781683508113 paperback
ISBN 9781683508120 eBook
Library of Congress Control Number: 2017916071

Cover Design by:
Rachel Lopez
r2cdesign.com

Cover illustration by:
Donna Murillo

Interior Design by:
Paul Curtis

In an effort to support local communities, raise awareness and funds, Morgan James Publishing donates a percentage of all book sales for the life of each book to Habitat for Humanity Peninsula and Greater Williamsburg.

Get involved today! Visit
www.MorganJamesBuilds.com

In Memory of Dave Clark
12th March 1937 to 14th June 2014
Love you and miss you always, Dad

ACKNOWLEDGEMENTS

Writing books can be a bit lonely, not to mention quite boring! Luckily, I had lots of company and love along the way and I want to thank my friends and family for all their support.

My husband, Brent, was a fantastic sounding-board, collaborator and editor and I love him heaps.

A massive 'thank you' to my mum Hazel, my dad David, my step-dad Michael – I am so proud of my mum who has always been incredibly supportive of me and I am thankful for her help and love. Also thanks to my brother, Russell, sister-in-law Jeab, and godmother Peggy – you have all always been there for me and I can't thank you enough. And a very special 'thank you' to my niece Erin Clark who inspired me so much that I wrote my first ever children's stories for her when she was busy growing up into the amazing, mature woman she is today.

Many people kindly donated their names to characters in this trilogy. Although the characters are nothing like the real people (and cat), I was proud to be able to honor them in this way. Thank you to Twinkle, Hazel and Michael Gibson, Dave Clark, LuAnne Underwood Autry, Peggy Lee Underwood Hornsby, Meera, Olive Saunders, Persis Clark, Don McConnochie, Muriel McConnochie, Heath and Nathan Matavuso-Lowe, Yvonne Tissington, Yvonne Lowe, Russell Clark and Ellie Tomsett. Oh, and one more 'thank' – thanks for lunch, Lile Ramsey!

I love the fabulous front cover of this book, don't you? It was designed by the very talented Donna Murillo of DHMDesign and I am grateful to her, and to Sarah Nisbet of Inkshed Editorial who did a brilliant first edit of this book.

I am extremely grateful to Wendy Busby who helped me understand dyslexic-readers and the character of Rory, and to Esther Whitehead,

Managing Trustee of the Dyslexic Foundation of New Zealand who was so helpful when I contacted her for advice.

I am very lucky and proud that this book was accepted by Morgan James Kids to be published. Many, many thanks to everyone there.

And finally, did you know that The Uncooperative Flying Carpet is the first book in a trilogy? All three books together are called The Strange Sagas of Sabrina Summers. It came from a short story I wrote for my stepdaughter when she was a little girl, and the character of Sabrina is inspired by her. This trilogy is dedicated to Steph McConnochie, love her lots.

However old you are, if you want to write a book or some short stories, then you can ask your friends and family for their support too.

PROLOGUE

It was a terrible day for a wedding. The rain slanted down by the bucket load, and stung the hands and faces of people hurrying down the street. The wind blew in sudden gusts and spiteful swirls. It caught at clothes and sent trash skidding along the street.

As the guests arrived, they had to hurry from their warm, dry cars along the slippery sidewalk, clutching their umbrellas and hats. The groom huddled in the doorway of the church, sheltering from the worst of the weather. He greeted people as they arrived, shaking their hands and smiling warmly. He was a tall man with sand-colored hair and gentle, blue eyes.

Across the street from the church was a small park with benches and trees. Behind a tree, a man was hiding. He was watching the chaos caused by the weather and loving it. Every time someone skidded on wet leaves, he laughed out loud. At one point, the church door banged in the wind and a small torrent of water was dislodged from the rain gutter, right onto the groom's shoes. The man had doubled over, he was laughing so hard.

Eventually, a long, white limousine drew up. Two children looked through the windows and a boy dressed in a suit jumped out. He was about eight years old and had vivid, carroty hair that stuck up all over the place like a hairy orange explosion on his head.

The boy looked very grumpy and sulky. He stuck his fingers inside his shirt collar and dramatically mimed choking to death, even dropping to his knees in a puddle. When he opened his mouth to wail, his two front teeth were missing. Next out of the car was a girl; she was taller than the boy and her hair was blonde, just like the groom's. In spite of their different coloring, you could tell by the way she tried to ignore him, and her "give-me-a- break" expression, that she was the boy's older sister. The girl was about twelve years old and wore a pink dress with a lot of ruffles. She kept yanking at the shiny skirt and wriggling as if she'd rather be wearing shorts and a sweatshirt. As soon as she was out of the car, her little brother tried to push her into the puddle. The man behind the tree couldn't hear what she yelled, but he smirked when the boy laughed then tried to stand on the hem of her long bridesmaid's dress.

"That's my boy, Rory," the man muttered.

At last the bride herself stepped out of the car and into the storm. The man's expression changed at once. His lip curled and his eyes narrowed, glowering at the woman. He stretched out his fingers and clawed them back into tight fists. This cold autumn weather made his hand ache, especially the scar where part of one of his fingers was missing. He pulled a tiny box from his pocket. It was wooden and had 'Property of WW' carved into the lid. He opened it and a white mist slipped out and swirled through the air, heading to the car.

As the man's fingers flickered, the mist grew into a malicious squall which swept around the bride, almost as if following the sweeping gestures he made. It whipped her white dress around her legs and tore the veil from her head so that it danced just beyond her stretching fingers. The veil hovered in the air like a ghost, before snagging on a nearby oak tree. He grinned, pleased with his work, then pocketed the box and pulled out a cream-colored piece of card. He read it for the hundredth time.

Sabrina & Rory Summers
invite you to the marriage
of their father, Dave Summers
to
Bridget Bishop
at Melas Chapel, Main St. Melas
on Friday 13th June at 2.00 pm

They hope you will be able to attend

"I guess it's show time," he said, as he threw the card to the ground and slipped his injured hand into his jacket pocket. Then he ripped the veil from the twigs that held it tight and walked across to the bride who was frantically patting her head. As he stepped out into the street, the rain eased off and the wind died down. His expression changed from malice to pleasant courtesy.

"I think this must be yours," he said, handing it to her. He was not sure, but as the bride thanked him, he thought he saw a glimmer of recognition in her eyes. She glanced down at his hand and he was glad he had hidden it in his coat pocket.

CHAPTER 1

I woke up with a face full of grass. It smelled lovely, actually. Fresh and, well, grassy. It tickled the inside of my nose. Then I wondered if there were worms in it, so I leapt to my feet swiping at my face and brushing bits of grass from my long, pink, ruffled dress.

From my what?

I looked down. Huh? This was my hideous and totally embarrassing bridesmaid's dress from last month. So why was I wearing it again now? Last thing I remembered was ... what? I put my hand on the back of my head to feel for bumps. Had I been in an accident? Had I fallen asleep at my dad's wedding and just dreamed the whole of the last month? If so, I needed to get more interesting dreams, because all I had dreamed about was going to school, doing my chores and being asleep. My fingers moved across my head. I could feel no bumps, so that was a good thing. What I could feel was that I had a strange wig on my head. The hair was totally different from mine. Mine is pretty long, like armpit long, but this was insanely long and it was in the most complicated arrangement of braids and swags anyone could imagine. I pulled some of it forward and looked. I'm blonde, but this was Blonde, capital B. And Long, capital L. It reached to my waist, even though it was draped and pinned up. I dropped it and carefully placed both hands on top of my head. There was a weird spiky thing growing out of the center of my skull.

Immediately I knew what had happened. This was obviously Rory's work. Somehow my little brother had sneaked into my bedroom at night, put a wig on my head, and dressed me in my bridesmaid's outfit. He was going to be in so much trouble when I got my hands on him. I heard a groan I recognized from behind me. I spun around to grab the little pest but stopped, arms outstretched when I saw my BFF, Persis Perkins, spread eagled on the ground next to Rory. What were they doing here? And while I was asking questions, where was "here" exactly?

Rory opened his eyes and wriggled until he was sitting up. He yawned and stretched, then struggled to stand up. He's always been hopeless at waking up. It's a family thing. He made little fists with his hands, ground them into his eyes, and started to yawn again. Mid- yawn, with his mouth wide open he happened to look over at me. His head slowly went down and then back up as he looked me over. Rory burst out laughing, pointed at me, and slapped theatrically at his leg, just to make sure that everyone understood I looked funny.

I've heard being an only child is great.

Meanwhile, Persis had also gotten to her feet and stood next to him. She was too busy staring at him to notice me. I've known her ever since we were at Melas Elementary School. We hit it off right away and always stood up for each other. She stood up for me again now.

"You don't look so great yourself, Rory," she told him firmly. He stopped laughing and looked down at himself. Now it was my turn to laugh and point. I checked him out and snort-laughed.

"Ohmygosh, those shoes," I gasped, hardly able to talk. Whoever had decided to dress me in a crumpled, pink marshmallow had really gone nuts with my brother. Rory's entire outfit was shiny. He wore a tunic shirt with big blousy sleeves, which was shiny and white. It was tucked into shiny blue pants that were so wide they flapped when he moved, but were tight around his ankles. A broad red cloth cinched him in at the waist and a buttonless vest completed his outfit.

Oh, and those shoes that made me laugh so much? On his feet he wore gold slippers encrusted with glittering pieces of mirror, which curled around from the toe like a pug dog's tail. They were incredibly exaggerated, and were surely never worn by people in real life. He bent down and started to tug at the shoes.

Next, I turned my attention to Persis herself.

"You got off lightly," I told her. She looked down at herself and nodded. She wore a plain, old-fashioned dress in blue and white check, and around her shoulders was a red cape with a hood.

"Yeah, I guess so, Brina," she answered. "But what I want to know is why are we dressed like this—and where are we?"

CHAPTER 2

"I don't know where we are," I answered. I was starting to wonder if we should be scared. This was a pretty weird situation after all.

"Why are we wearing these clothes?" Rory grunted. He was now sitting on the ground, with one leg waggling in the air, as he yanked at the curling toe of his right slipper. He looked up at me as he spoke.

Persis looked at me.

I looked at them. I shrugged. I had no idea. Why were they even looking at me? How would I know? Were we safe? Were we in danger? Were all three of us having the same crazy dream?

Whatever was happening to us, at least we were all together. Nothing is as frightening when you have someone else with you, I always think. That was why ... oh dear, something was coming back to me. I remembered talking Persis into come along with me to do something—something that I couldn't quite remember—because I was scared to do it by myself. Now she was in as much trouble as I was.

"Well, the last thing I remember was ..." I wrinkled up my face and tried to bully my brain into working properly.

"I know," Persis said. "We'd, uh, we'd decided to follow your stepmom to see where she had been sneaking off to." She cast a glance at Rory, to see if he remembered the same thing. He was red in the face and sweating as he struggled with his shoe, but still heard her.

"That's right," he piped up as he rolled from one side to the other, now with both legs in the air and one hand on each foot. He paused to gather his breath and glanced up from where he lay. "You said, 'I'm telling you, Persis, there's something weird about Bridget'," he said. Persis and I rounded on him in unison, our knuckles on our hips.

"We were following Bridget," I said to him. "We. So what about you?" He didn't care that we were angry at him for eavesdropping. He had other things to worry about. He started to drag the heels of his glittering slippers across the grass, gouging channels in the earth.

"I," he mimicked, "I was following you following Bridget," he explained.

All right, now we were getting somewhere. It seemed that my friend and I decided to follow my new stepmom because ... because why? Then I remembered. It had all started after Bridget herself had sneaked out of our house. But then I remembered something else: I had been officially grounded when I had followed her. Oops.

My thinking was interrupted.

"RRRRrrrrrrrrr!" Rory screamed out. He lay on his back and pummelled the ground beneath him with his clenched fists and smashed his feet up and down. "I HATE THESE CLOTHES!" he screeched; his face was scarlet and his eyes were bulging. "GET THESE CLOTHES OFF ME!" he continued, with tears streaming from his eyes.

Persis and I wandered over to him and took a foot each. We talked over Rory as we began to wiggle his slippers, speaking louder to make ourselves heard over the wails and howls of his current tantrum.

"Hey, I think I was grounded; do you remember that?" I asked.

Persis nodded, and started pulling instead of wiggling. "Yeah, that's right. Something to do with being rude to your stepmom, wasn't it?"

I nodded and joined her in the pulling.

"Mmm, yes, it was." We moved to stand next beside one another, each of us holding a foot. We crouched to steady our legs, leaned back, and pulled with all our might. There was a terrific thump as we both pulled so hard that we flew backward a whole yard and landed on our behinds. We each had a slipper in our hands and as we sat up, we grinned and high-fived using the shoes instead of our hands. Then we looked at Rory, expecting to see his cheesy feet and hear a 'thanks guys.'

Instead Rory's feet were waving in the air, still shod in the golden, glittering slippers, which winked and twinkled in the sunshine. I looked at the shoe in my hand and as I stared, it turned to dust.

Icky! I flicked my hands and brushed them clean on my dress. It looked like whatever we did, we were stuck with these clothes and this hair until we managed to get back home.

Home. The word set me thinking. We'd already been through enough, and it wasn't fair that Rory and I had even more to deal with.

Dad, Rory and I had been by ourselves since my mom left us, just after Rory was born. That was even before any of us knew what a pest he could be; back then, he was just a cute, helpless baby. One day she was there, the next she wasn't. Weeks and weeks later, her older brother— our wonderful Uncle Don—had come to the house. He had introduced himself to Dad and then he gave us the terrible news. Mom had sent him an email. She had left us. She had simply decided that being a parent and a wife weren't enough for her, and that she wanted to be free. Of course, I was only four years old so I don't remember any of this, and Dad would never talk about it, but last year, Uncle Don sat down with Rory and me and said we deserved to know the truth. Boy, that was some afternoon!

Uncle Don sat on the edge of my bed. Rory sat on his lap, his arms wrapped around Uncle Don's neck. He had always been fascinated by our uncle's thick, auburn mustache. He kept trying to reach for it, but Uncle Don brushed his hands away.

"So, tell us about her, please Uncle Don," I said. "Dad won't be back for hours. Please. We want to know."

"All right, Sabrina, if you're sure."

Rory and I both nodded. We were sure. We had a right to know what had happened, didn't we? Was it us? Was it Dad? He could be kind of a nag; maybe he drove her away.

"Well, kids, you know I love you both, right?"

Sure, we knew. Uncle Don came and went because of his job, but he always brought us presents and played with us when he was around. We nodded.

"Well, I love my sister, too. But the truth is, she was always kind of unreliable," he had said. "She never stuck to anything for long. She rebelled against our family, broke our parents' hearts." He shook his head, twirling the ends of his great gingery mustache. "It was nothing to do with you, or your dad, it was all her. We always knew she would come to a sad end."

I felt my eyes fill with tears—they knew to cry before my mind did. "After that first email I didn't hear from her for months afterward, then I got the bad news. She had died while she was away." Uncle Don's voice cracked as he spoke and then trailed away to silence.

I don't know about Rory, but I had always hoped something exciting had happened to Mom, like she was really a secret agent and only pretending to be dead.

"What happened to her?" I asked in a very quiet voice.

"Well, Sabrina, it seems that she was sailing a boat alone, hit bad weather, fell overboard, and drowned. The life jacket was still on board. Reckless ... she was always so reckless." He retreated into himself, taking a quiet moment. We didn't ask about anything more. We didn't want to know anything more.

Rory cried for three days afterward but I felt kind of sorry for Uncle Don, too. He told us the worst day of his life had been when he had to tell Dad that Mom had died in a boating accident. He tried to make us feel better by saying that neither of us were anything like her.

Then he had clapped Rory hard on his back and said, "Cheer up, my boy. I will bring you back a cuckoo clock from my tour of Europe." He rose to his feet and towered above us, before ruffling our hair and pulling candy from behind our ears.

"Smoke and mirrors, kids," he said whenever we asked him how he did his tricks. "Magic is just all smoke and mirrors."

We had watched him leave from my bedroom window, still a little dazed from what he had told us and the vigorous hair-ruffling. The words "The Great Donaldo" were painted on the side of his huge RV. Uncle Don was a traveling magician who put on shows all around the world, and was, without question, the best and coolest uncle ever.

Well, now you know that my dad was a widow and used to be a single parent. That's why he went on the Internet to find a new wife for himself and a stepmom for Rory and me: the stepmom we had all been following when we ended up in this mess.

CHAPTER 3

"Oh Dad, no way can you wear that to your date," I had wailed in horror.

The whole Internet dating thing hadn't worked out so well for Dad.

He was kind of innocent; and he was certainly not aware of how mean and greedy some of the women he met could be. Luckily, the "people-repellent" that is my little brother Rory saw most of the unsuitable applicants off. There were several who were quite a bit older than Dad: a little older than our grandma to be honest! Then there was one who didn't know that soap and hot water had been invented and who smelled so bad the neighboring farm had telephoned us to ask if our drains were blocked. There were a couple of cacklers who laughed like hyenas all the time; one who wanted Dad to send Rory and me away to boarding school; three who asked to see Dad's bank account and then left pretty quickly afterward; and finally, there was Bridget Bishop.

Rory had a few different techniques he liked to use if he didn't like one of the women Dad was trying to date. Eating three cans of baked beans before being introduced was especially effective. Or he would pretend he was a pet cat and would try to curl up on their laps. My personal favorite was the moment when he screamed loudly right in the face of the woman who smelled like drains.

So when we saw Bridget's profile online and listened in when Dad talked to her on the phone, we were actually pleased that someone who seemed nice and normal was interested in our dad. We were tired of all the dates and we wanted it to be over.

That's why I was so anxious that my dad did not wear a zip-up sweater with a pattern of yellow-and-green diamonds down the front.

Well, amazingly, I was wrong; Bridget came to the house that first time and told Dad he looked extremely handsome, and that the green diamonds brought out the flecks of green in his eyes.

He proposed to her two months later and they were married three more months after that. My head stopped swirling only long enough to realize that I was being forced to wear a pink dress which looked like the covers that old ladies use to hide their spare rolls of toilet paper underneath.

Before we could blink, Rory and I had a new stepmother. Wow. They had fallen for each other almost at first sight—just like that. It would have been romantic if they hadn't been so old and, you know, he wasn't my dad. At first, it was pretty much okay. Bridget moved into the house, and we all had gotten used to each other and worked out new routines. Bridget began to talk about a separate bathroom for the grown-ups pretty quickly; but yes, it was okay.

Overall.

Well, maybe a few teething problems.

Especially her cooking. That caused us a few teething problems. Rory in particular had to cut up his food very small because there was no way he could bite into it with his two front teeth missing. And she had kind of a weakness for stews and casseroles and soups, or anything she could cook in one big black pot. But they all tasted the same: like sweaty socks. And looked the same: like melted soap with cut-up sweaty socks floating in it. Unfortunately, Rory could eat that kind of food with no problems, so she made it often. But the main thing was that my dad was happy. When they got married, Bridget had given up her job as a librarian over in Manchester-by-the-Sea and her home in Singing Beach, so she had plenty of free time to look after the house and Rory and me. That meant she made us do our homework; and our grades went up, which was quite a surprise. She sang around the house and brought inside bunches of wild flowers and herbs, and also what I secretly thought were weeds, but I didn't like to upset her. For the first time, Persis was allowed to come for sleepovers, now that there was a responsible adult female in the house. And Rory slept better at night.

Unfortunately there were a few things that worried me—a few little niggles that led us to follow her that fateful evening, and meant that we wound up in some field we didn't recognize with the strangest Halloween outfits on.

CHAPTER 4

"Huuurrrggh!"

The gross sound distracted me from the effort of remembering exactly what had happened. We all looked at each other, wondering what it was.

"Huuuurrrggh!" The noise happened again. Persis pointed toward a large tree, which stood alone in the corner of the field. From one side of the trunk peeped someone's backside, covered in tattered, gray fabric with square patches of bright material sewn on in great, looping stitches.

"Someone's there," I whispered. The expressions on Rory's and Persis' faces clearly said, "Well, duh; of course there's someone there".

"I think they're puking," I added softly. "What shall we do?" I asked.

I was about to suggest sneaking away, but I was too late. At the suggestion of being able to watch someone throwing up, Rory had hurried over toward the tree.

"Oh, hey; what's going on? Why is it that color?" I heard his clear young voice ring out. Oh dear. I figured we had better catch up with him. He was so annoying to everyone he met that I was used to stepping in to rescue people from him or to save him from being beaten up.

"Oh, hi," he was continuing. "It's you. What are you doing here?"

I caught Persis' eye. Someone we knew? It must be Bridget. Yes, that's right, I remembered something else. We had followed my stepmom to the field that lay on the other side of the dirt road in front of our house.

We ran over to Rory, and the figure behind the tree stood up, swiping at her mouth with the back of her hand. She was smaller than Persis and me, quite dainty with very pale skin, big brown eyes with long, dark eyelashes and a mass of shiny brown hair tied up in a ragged gray band.

Oh no.

Not her.

Anyone but her.

Not Olive Amanda Ayres, my arch-enemy at school. Not old "Ayres and Graces" herself. What was she doing here? She looked at us. We looked at her. Then she burst out laughing as she checked us out.

I looked her up and down and wondered why she was laughing at us when she looked like that. Mind you, I had no idea what I looked like.

Okay then, this had stopped being funny. We all had some weird clothes on, and although we could see each other, none of us knew what we looked like head to toe. I wanted to see how I looked, and I especially wanted to know what was growing out of my head. I looked around the field. Now that I was taking the time, it seemed to be about the same size and shape as the field by our house. Just a boring stretch of grass with a couple of trees for shading the horse that lived there. That meant that over near the hedge, there should have been a large, black, plastic barrel, which was used for storing water for the horse to drink. We would be able to see our reflections in there; and after seeing herself, Olive would have no reason to laugh at me—yet again—because of the clothes I wore.

I crooked my right index finger at them to get them to follow me, and without waiting to see if they would, I hurried across to the corner of the field. I was saved the embarrassment of being ignored, because they all tagged along behind me. I could hear Olive's voice asking questions all the way across, buzzing like a whiney hornet in my ear. I blocked out her voice, an important skill that I acquired after becoming a big sister. We each needed to see for ourselves what we looked like.

Huh? That's odd, I thought to myself—and definitely not for the last time that day. The plastic water barrel had been replaced by a long, low stone trough for horses to drink from. Still, it was full of clear water that reflected blue sky with fluffy white clouds scudding across it. But that was odd too, because when we had followed Bridget, it had been early evening— hadn't it? Now it was the middle of the day.

We stood in a row, shuffled forward, and stared at our images reflected in the flat water. Horror dawned on each of our faces.

Persis' brown eyes widened in alarm, and she clapped a hand to her mouth. Her long, curly black hair had been tightly plaited so that there was one braid on each side of her head. The red cape and hood looked good against her dark skin, but I could tell that she hated the hair. She started to pull off the red polka-dot ribbons that were tied at the bottom of each braid.

Rory saw his reflection and his ginger freckles almost popped right off his face. He began to tear at his shiny vest.

Me? I saw the spiky thing, and realized it was not a strange growth but a tiny crown covered in sparkling gems. As I had thought, I was wearing my bridesmaid's dress although it seemed to have extra swags, and even a small train at the back. The worst thing was my hair. It had always grown quickly, but this was ridiculous. It was thicker, blonder, and at least eight inches longer. I blinked and looked again, then shook my head. Had it grown even longer while my eyes were shut? I touched it with one hesitant hand. It was elaborately styled on the top of my head, and then it spilled down my back. I tried to yank off the crown.

"Yeowch!" I squealed. It was very much attached to my scalp.

The only one who actually cried was Olive. She took one look at her dirt-smeared face, untidy, mousy brown hair, ragged dress, and bare feet—and wept.

CHAPTER 5

I couldn't blame her. She had been adding chestnut and golden tints to her hair for the past two years, and she always wore the most expensive clothes to school. She had top-of-the- range electronic devices, lived in the nicest part of town, and was without doubt the meanest girl in my grade.

"L-l-look at m-m-me," she sobbed. "I ... I look like Cinderella!" she wailed.

I ignored her. Firstly, I had problems of my own. All that heavy hair was giving me a headache. Secondly, Olive had picked on me from my first week at Melas Middle School, so why should I care? Melas is a small town in Massachusetts, so there's no escaping your schoolyard enemies, although this was taking things a bit too far.

"She's right," Persis said, throwing her ribbons to the ground and untwining the braids. Oh yes, she was right. Olive did look like Cinderella, but there was more to this. I turned to Persis.

"You, I told her, "look like Little Red Riding Hood." "And me? I look like Rapunzel." I looked at poor Rory; his vivid hair was sticking out at all angles and his face was crimson as he stomped up and down on his vest until it too, turned to dust and drifted away on the wind.

"And Rory looks like Ali Baba," I finished.

Olive bent over the trough and scooped water onto her face, trying to wash off the cinder smears.

"Uh, Olive?" I said. She glared at me, her face dripping.

"What?" she hissed.

"That's for horses to drink out of," I explained. "So you are basically washing your face in horse saliva," I added, with a tiny, quiet snigger that

I hope she didn't hear. Olive is the class drama queen, even worse than me, and she sank to her knees, arched her back, and flung her arms wide.

"Nooooooo!" she shrieked, to the field in general.

"Neigggghhh," came the reply.

Where there are horses' drinking troughs, there are horses. This particular horse was called Clyde. Clyde was a huge brown and white Clydesdale horse with a shaggy white mane and tail, and white-fringed hooves. He had lived in the field by our house since we moved in. He was very friendly, and when we were little, Dad used to take Rory and me across the track to feed him apples. Unfortunately, the apples didn't agree with him. He used to break wind dramatically, which always sent Rory into gales of laughter.

In one way it wasn't a surprise to see our old friend, Clyde. We had started our strange journey in his field, after all. But it was a massive surprise to see that a unicorn's horn had sprouted from his forehead. The horn gleamed in the sunshine, reflecting sparkling rainbows of pastel colors. He neighed again and shook his head, then muscled in among us and began to drink, just at the spot where Olive had been splashing water on her face. I heard her give a little whimper.

As Rory and I had grown older, we had outgrown Clyde, and often didn't go to visit him for weeks on end. But Bridget hadn't forgotten him. From the moment she met Dad and started to call at our house, she had gone to visit with Clyde. She didn't just fuss over him, though, like we had. She stood face to face with him and had long, involved chats with him. When I had watched them, Clyde had nodded his great head, stamped his feet, and whinnied or neighed, which are all typical horse things to do, or it would have looked for all the world as if he was answering her.

However, it was when she started taking books to the field and reading to him that I thought something mighty strange was going on with my new stepmom. I mean, I know she was a librarian and always had a book, or an e-book on a device, with her, but this was very strange behavior.

But it was when I caught her whispering over one of her pots of stew that I really started to have suspicions about Bridget Bishop Summers.

CHAPTER 6

Back only a few short months ago, when Dad had first introduced us to Bridget Bishop, she had seemed normal.

She had curly brown hair and was quite short for an adult (she used to ask me to reach things down from high shelves for her). She probably liked snacking on cookies while sitting on the sofa a whole lot more than she liked jogging and yogurt. When we met her, she worked as a librarian in Manchester-by-the-Sea and she usually wore boring black dresses with white collars. She had pink skin, which always looked freshly scrubbed, and she had one melting-chocolate brown eye and one sky-blue eye. She told us it was a syndrome called iris heterochromia and it was just the way the pigments in her eyes had formed. All we heard her say was, "Blah blah blah blah." She could see perfectly well, she had explained, but it sometimes gave Rory and me an odd feeling when we looked at her. On the day of the wedding, Dad's side of the church was full of friends and neighbors and relations. Persis came along and had given me a big thumbs up when she saw my dress. Rory's friends Heath and Nathan were there too, giggling and hiding under the pews. But Bridget's side of the church was almost empty—there were just three people from the library.

Uncle Don had been Dad's best man of course, and he had kept on looking over at all the empty seats and shaking his head as if he couldn't believe how unpopular Dad's new wife was. He was too well-mannered to say anything of course, but his expression made me start to wonder if we should have asked Bridget a few questions about her past before we let her marry our dad.

Another strange thing was the way she acted right through the ceremony. The whole time she kept glancing behind her at the doors, as if she expected someone to come bursting through. When the priest asked if anyone knew of any reason that the wedding should not go ahead, I definitely saw her cross her fingers.

We could have gotten used to the pots full of weeds and wild flowers around the house, and even the fact that she read out loud to a horse; but let's face it, Rory was never, ever going to wear a crystal around his neck to "protect him from evil" and I was not happy to find salt poured in a neat line along the window ledge in my bedroom. When I asked her why, she seemed embarrassed and mumbled something about keeping out bad spirits.

When Uncle Don came to dinner one evening, he casually asked Bridget about herself. He asked about her family and where she grew up. She got flustered and muddled, and then "accidentally" threw her plate of sweaty-socks stew on the floor to cause a diversion.

As he was about to leave that evening, Uncle Don pulled me to one side and bent down to whisper in my ear.

"Sabrina, if that woman ever frightens or harms your brother or you, you must call me right away. I'll get here as fast as I can." His earnest expression sent shivers up my spine, and that night I locked my bedroom door for the first time in my entire life.

The next afternoon, I caught her heading out of the back door with a large, old leather- bound book in her hands. Uncle Don's words were still rattling around in my brain.

"Where are you going?" I demanded.

Dad glanced up from the crossword he was doing.

"Just, you know ..." her voice trailed off.

"Tell me. I want to know," I insisted. "Where is it you sneak off to all the time?"

Then a terrible thought seeped into my brain and came out of my mouth as real, spoken words before I could stop them.

"Are you meeting another man?"

She gasped. Dad gasped and slammed down his newspaper. I got grounded for being disrespectful.

And that is why Persis and I were following my stepmom to a field one summer afternoon the following weekend, even though I was grounded. Rory had sneaked out to follow us, which he often did because he's a royal pain. But it didn't tell us where Bridget was now. Nor why Olive was there. And we still had no idea why we were no longer in Melas and were dressed like characters from a child's book of fairy tales.

CHAPTER 7

Although I had no idea where to start with most of my questions, at least I could find out why Olive was there. I swung around to face her. She looked just as dirty and her hair was just as tangled as if she hadn't tried to clean herself up.

Hmm. I had seen her sloshing the water all over her face and scrubbing with her fists. There should have been some difference at least.

I glanced over at Persis. She was standing, watching us. She had picked up the ribbons from the ground and was absentmindedly twirling one of them in her fingers. She obviously didn't realize that her hair was tightly braided again and the red polka-dot ribbons had been replaced with yellow tartan ones. Rory had slumped to the ground, and was leaning his back against the cool stone of the trough, ignoring the water that Clyde's enthusiastic drinking was flicking over him. He wore another shiny vest, this time in bottle green. In his hands were the ragged remains of his first vest.

Ah, I began to understand. Great. In fact, wonderful. Apparently we were stuck with the outfits we had on, and no matter how we tried, we weren't able to take them off. At least not until we figured out what was happening and where we were. Okay, we would just have to live with it for now.

"Olive," I began, trying to be nice through gritted teeth. "What are you doing here?"

She stared at me as if I was insane, her mouth hanging open. I wished I could take a photo of her on my cell phone. Oh, of course. Without waiting for her to reply, I slapped the palm of my hand against my forehead. What was I thinking? We girls surely all had our smartphones with us. We could look up where we were, and then call Dad for help.

I blinked; smacking my own head had hurt.

I started patting up and down my dress, looking for my phone. Nothing. This frilly nightmare didn't even have a pocket. I looked back to where I had woken up in case the phone had fallen there when I did. Nothing.

"Phones!" I yelled. "Check to see if you have your phone with you." Everyone did the same funny dance as I just had, jumping around and patting their arms and legs. A full minute of hope and excitement was replaced with the gloom and despair we had felt before my brainwave.

"What do you mean 'what am I doing here'?" Olive demanded, carrying on from where I had left off. She took a step closer to me, and looked very angry and upset.

"Where exactly is 'here'? Do you know?" she yelled. "This is all your fault. You're so dumb that you bring everyone to some place and don't even know where it is. And why are we in these clothes?" She took another step closer. I could see her eyes were narrowed and her mouth was screwed up tight. She was furious.

I stepped backward.

"Um, Sabrina?" said Persis.

"How should I know where we are?" I shouted back, ignoring Persis. "We were just following my stepmom and all of a sudden this happened. Why were you even in our field?" I demanded.

She took another step toward me. I took another step back. "Sabrina? Brina?" Persis pestered me again.

"Your field? That's a laugh," scoffed Olive. "It's my father's field. He owns all the land along there. I was taking a look at it for him because he's thinking of putting a sewage processing plant there. Although ..." she continued, taking another step and forcing me back again, "...

although I think the smell from your house will be even worse than from the plant," she finished spitefully.

Uh-oh.

As I took another pace away from her, I suddenly realized what Persis had been warning me about. I felt a low stone object against the back of my legs. My arms waved wildly about in the air, I toppled backward into the drinking trough, and plopped down—right in the water.

CHAPTER 8

Clyde was not impressed with finding me in his drinking water: I could tell. His long horn poked me in the ribs as Persis pulled me out, and Olive and Rory cried with laughter.

The dress was even more uncomfortable and heavy when it was soaking wet. I twisted around and squeezed the wet fabric until my hands ached and it was only damp instead of sodden.

Rory had recovered enough to talk by then. At least my falling into the trough had cheered him up and stopped his mega-tantrum. In fact, he felt so much better that he asked the obvious question.

"Where's Bridget?" he wanted to know.

Where indeed was Bridget Bishop Summers?

"Who's Bridget?" asked Olive. Just as I was about to tell her to mind her own business, Rory told her all about our dad being a solo parent, about him marrying Bridget, and about how strange she was. He stood right next to Olive and gazed adoringly at her. Well, that was going to make this day even better—not. My little brother was developing a crush on my schoolyard enemy.

"So we all followed her when she sneaked out of the house," he explained. "She was carrying a sack with some things in, and a big book."

Oh, that was it. I remembered now. Persis and I had stood behind the apple tree where Olive had been throwing up. Hmm, we would have to remember to be careful where we stood on the way back, then. We had watched Bridget, although it was difficult to see much through the leaves without sticking our heads right out into the open. She had taken three or four items out of the sack and laid them on the ground next to Clyde, and then she seemed to be singing or chanting. I had started to giggle but then we saw her raise a stick as if she was going to hit Clyde with it.

We had raced over to stop her, then ... BAM! There had been smoke and flashes of light and I remembered being swirled around and around like water going down a sink. No wonder Olive had been ill; I had felt pretty nauseous myself. I felt the same way a yo-yo must feel.

"Hmmm," said Olive thoughtfully. "I didn't see any of this. I'd just come in through the gate and didn't even have time to see that you guys were there." She pinched her bottom lip between her forefinger and thumb. "So she laid objects on the ground, she was chanting, and she had a big book and a stick?"

I nodded.

"Well, I'd say it was obvious, wouldn't you?"

Persis and Rory both nodded, but this time I didn't. I had no idea what Ayres and Graces was talking about.

"So obvious," they chorused. "Why didn't we see it before?" they added, rubbing it in. They saw the expression of complete "I don't know what's going on" on my face.

"Your stepmother is a witch," Olive explained, speaking very slowly to make sure I understood it this time.

Oh of course, I totally saw. Huh? What? No way, a witch? But there was no wart, no pointy hat—and she had never once tried to eat us.

"I expect witches come in all shapes and sizes," said Olive, who was acting as though she was suddenly an expert on witches.

Hard as I tried to think of another, more rational, reason for what had happened, I just couldn't.

My stepmom was a witch, and somehow she had magicked us into a strange land and then she had vanished and left us to fend for ourselves. This was going to make for an interesting "What I did at the weekend" essay for school.

"So now what?" Persis asked me.

"I've no idea," I told her. "What does everyone else think?" Three round, bald faces and one long, hairy face turned toward me. Four sets of eyes looked at me expectantly.

"What?" I asked. "Why are you all looking at me?"

"She's your stepmom," said Olive.

"This was your idea," added Persis.

"You're the oldest," chipped in Rory.

"Paaarrp!" was Clyde's contribution.

Whew! He had definitely been eating apples recently.

Then he put his head down and nudged me gently with the tip of his horn. He seemed to be suggesting something. He lifted his head and pointed his horn toward the far side of the field. I followed the direction he was pointing with my gaze, and noticed that there was a gap in the hedge that surrounded the field.

I glanced around me, looked at the ragtag group of people (and a unicorn) that I was with, and sighed.

"Well, I guess we need to find Bridget," I said. "And Clyde thinks we should go that way; so that's the way we will go."

CHAPTER 9

Before we headed off, though, I took a moment, just for myself. The others were following Clyde, and I let them all go in front of me. There were two reasons for this. One was that I needed to gather my thoughts and try to figure out what was going on here. The other was that I didn't want to be too close behind Clyde when he had been eating apples.

"Okay, Sabrina, think," I told myself. There was no way that any of this was real, of course. I mean, things like magic spells don't actually happen outside of books and movies. But then, why did it all seem so natural to me? That was strange in itself. Surely I should be afraid, I thought to myself. A normal reaction would be to freak out, wouldn't it? I should have been panicking and running around in circles screaming, but I felt as if I was taking it all in my stride. Just another day in Weirdsville. I concluded that if I could remember some of the details it would help everything fall into place.

I concentrated. The memory of what had happened to me, to us all, started to drift back now. I had been crouching behind the tree with Persis, and I had almost jumped out of my skin with fright when Rory had snuck up on us and whispered "boo" in our ears. I had grabbed him by his superhero t-shirt and yanked him down to crouch alongside us girls. Of course, how could I have forgotten?

"What's going on?" he had said, much too loudly for my liking. Persis, who for reasons I will never ever understand, had a soft spot for my pesky little brother. I was about to ignore his question and send him back home, but she told him that we were following Bridget. He seemed a bit hesitant, but the memory of being grounded was still hot and vivid to me. So I made it very clear to him that he had better not tell on me, and if he had any sense, he'd stick with us. We were all going to find out what she was up to and then go back and tell Dad.

I gave a little sigh. I wasn't proud of forcing Rory to stay with us, especially not now. So it was my fault that both Rory and Persis were here. And I was starting to think that it was up to me to get them both back home.

When we had rushed over to stop Bridget hitting Clyde with a stick, a tiny puff of smoke had drifted from the tip of Bridget's stick and had started to swirl around her and Clyde, like a soft, purple-gray tornado that sparkled in the late-afternoon sun. It sent out little tendrils of smoke and as we ran into them, they reached out for us and pulled us into its whirling center. It felt as though gentle fingers were reaching out and gripping our clothes and hair and ankles. And it seemed that it had somehow reached far enough to pull Olive into in with the rest of us.

The coils of smoke pulled our feet from under us and swung our legs into the air, and our bodies had floated above the ground for three long seconds. Then we were swept around and around, like bathwater running into a plug hole. A smell like boiled cabbages had filled our nostrils. Where the smoke touched our skin, it scraped like a dry rough sponge. It filled our mouths, making us cough; and our minds, making us dizzy. It had choked the air from our lungs and the sense from our brains. It swept us faster and higher until our worlds went black.

Then, sometime later, we had woken up. Some of us felt worse than others, but we were all in one piece. We had awakened in a strange land, in strange clothes, with no cell phones, and only the pointing horn of a farting Clydesdale unicorn to give us any idea of where to go. We had no idea what language people spoke, no money, and no knowledge of local transport or customs. In short, if anyone was going to freak out, it should have been me. But I felt strangely serene.

As it turned out, I should have gone with the "freaking out" option.

CHAPTER 10

I turned my face toward the direction in which Clyde had pointed, and started to follow the others. I took three paces and tripped over my own hair. I tutted, and then hooked it over my arm and carried it like an unwanted coat on a warm day.

I caught up with everyone and it seemed to be going okay for couple of minutes, but one of us was struggling already and wanted to make sure that everyone else knew it.

Step.

"Ouch."

Step.

"Ouch."

Step.

"Ouch."

Olive wasn't as shy as me about making a fuss. She had no shoes, just like Cinderella in the old fairy tale, but she had soft, modern feet. Each step she took hurt her.

It took her only three steps before she sat down and refused to move. I looked down at her and seriously considered leaving her behind—I thought it would be a lot easier in the long run. But instead, I heard my voice being supportive.

"Come on, you can do it," I told her. "There might be a shoe shop somewhere," I suggested. Her face did brighten at the thought of shoe shopping, and she even started to get up; but then, just as she had so often at school, Olive outwitted me.

"Great, you can bring me some back, then. I'll wait here," she said, with a smirk.

Amazingly, Rory had my back. He used the one simple magic word guaranteed to get her back up and walking with us.

"Alone?" he asked. Olive looked around her. None of us had any idea where we were and what kind of people lived here. We had already seen a unicorn, so pretty much anything could be hiding behind the hedge. No, there was no way she was going to stay there all by herself. Then she looked at my feet. I could tell she was checking to see if my shoes would fit her, and then I would get to walk barefoot. For the first time I was glad to have big, wide feet and the pink sneakers that I loved and wore every day with every outfit were way too large for her. These shoes were as much a part of me as my teeth. For the first time in my life, I was thankful for inheriting my big feet from Dad.

She quickly dismissed Rory's slippers, although I think that if he could have gotten rid of them, he would have been happy to be shoeless. Then she turned toward Persis: but Persis had vanished.

We yelled and searched for her until we found her on the far side of the field, singing to herself and scooping up great bunches of wild flowers. She had a wicker basket with her now, although I had no idea where she found it, and she was placing the flowers into it. She kept dancing away from the narrow pathway that led across the field—the pathway that we were supposed to be following.

Of course. Little Red Riding Hood had strayed from the path through the woods to pick wild flowers. I sighed. This was going to be a very long and tiresome journey. Clyde eventually solved the problem for us. He knelt down beside Olive, and let her scramble onto his back, while holding onto his shaggy mane for balance.

"Okay, let's try again, people," I said.

We were off. I strode ahead, Rory scurried behind me, Persis mostly stayed with us although she kept darting off, and Olive on Clyde brought up the rear.

There was a good reason for Olive and Clyde to be at the rear of our little procession. Clyde had been snacking on apples while we had talked, and the aftereffects were noisy and smelly. And frequent.

At the edge of the field we climbed over a low wooden stile. Clyde stepped over it as if it was a log on the ground. We found ourselves on a narrow roadway made from crushed yellowy stones and pebbles. In the far distance, we saw an old-fashioned road sign. It had four finger-shaped boards, with writing on them, which all pointed in different directions.

Awesome! We would soon know where we were.

CHAPTER 11

We hurried up the road to read the sign, although I had to drag Persis away from an enticing woodpile—enticing to Persis, that is—with a hatchet buried deep in one of the logs. It lay near the signpost on the edge of the crossroads where we were standing.

"Stop it," I hissed at her. She raised her palms up and let them drop to her sides again.

"I can't help it," she said, looking mournful. "I just keep wanting to get an axe and chop things." Suddenly she looked very fierce. "There had better not be any wolves around here, that's all I can say," she added through clenched teeth.

Oh great. I hadn't even thought of natural threats, such as wild animals. I pushed an image of great white fangs, drool, and orange eyes away, and read the sign.

Nailed onto the middle was a piece of wood shaped like a crown. The background was painted blue, the crown part was painted gold, and the writing underneath was black.

You are now in the Kingdom of Dralfynia

said the sign. Below it were the words:

We welcome careful ox-cart drivers

So, now we knew where we were. Somewhere called "Dralfynia", though we still didn't know where that was exactly. And we also knew that we had come back to the olden days where there were no cars or buses: just carts pulled by huge cows. I thought about it. Probably no TV or Internet. Then a terrible thought hit me. Probably no toilet paper either.

Olive read out the rest of the signs.

"We could go to Timaru which is that way," she said, pointing ahead of us. There was one sign for each of the four roads at the crossroads, and her arm followed the direction that each place name was pointing in. "Or Lake Pleasant that way, or the town of Tylwyth Teg the way we've just come from, and of course Scary Forest over there."

She looked down on us from her perch on Clyde's broad back.

"I say we give Scary Forest a miss," she suggested. I might not have wanted to agree with her just from habit, but she was right. Somewhere named Scary Forest did not sound promising.

Since I couldn't pronounce "the town of Tylwyth Teg" without spitting, and a lake didn't sound like it would have much in the way of accommodation or food or people to help us, I suggested Timaru. The writing on the Timaru sign was the largest, which hopefully meant that it was a big city. I wished there were numbers to tell us how far away each place was.

Olive was nodding.

"I agree," she said. "What do you think, Rory?"

He didn't answer. Rory didn't bother to read signs that weren't friendly to dyslexics. Besides, he was too busy. He was standing with one foot on the tip of the other shoe, trying to straighten out his shiny slippers. In the meantime, Persis had sneaked over to the heap of logs with the axe and was standing on the woodpile trying to yank it out.

She had never been a very girly girl. In fact, she was a sporty tomboy, to tell the truth. But this desire to become a lumberjack was getting beyond a joke.

We heard a creaking sound, followed by a pop, a yell of triumph, and a panicked scream. Persis had torn the axe from the woodpile, but then she had cartwheeled backward and landed on her back; she was still clutching the small hatchet as sticks fell onto her. She jumped to her feet and ran toward us, brandishing the axe.

"Guys, guys, guys!" she shouted. "Look what I got!" I'd never seen her so happy. Then her eyes glittered and she crouched down, her eyes darting around, as if seeing danger everywhere. "Now I can protect you from those darned wolves," she hissed. Somehow, a twelve-year-old with an axe she had never used before didn't seem like much protection. Probably she was more of a threat to herself, but she was happy with her hatchet so we let her keep it.

When we set off this time, we found we all had a spring in our step. We knew where we were going—Timaru—and we knew where we were—in the kingdom of Dralfynia.

Everything would be fine, I felt certain. We walked off toward the sinking sun, enjoying the way that it tinted everything pink. We felt calm, happy—and completely unaware of the dangers that were facing us as we walked in totally the wrong direction.

Behind us, a gust of wind skittered along the lane, which not only sent pebbles and dust bunnies racing along, but also turned the sign back the way it should have pointed all along.

We were not walking to Timaru. We were headed right for Scary Forest.

CHAPTER 12

We walked.

And we walked.

And we walked.

We walked past fields full of tufty, rounded haystacks with little white canvas squares on top. They looked like handkerchiefs tied onto the top of a bald person's head.

We walked past fields full of crops and saw heaps of pumpkins piled high where they had been harvested. We walked past fields full of cows, sheep, and goats. Rory insisted on trying to talk to the animals in each field, just in case they were magic and could answer him. They stared at him blankly though he did get a few moos, baas and bleats.

In fact, we heard a lot of bleating on this boring journey, but almost all of it was from Olive. She complained incessantly about how uncomfortable poor Clyde's back was, about how itchy her dress made from rags was, and about how hungry she was.

She had a point with the last one though. We were all hungry, and we were all tired. It was starting to get dark and, even though we were together and nobody said it out loud, we were beginning to be afraid. The shock and amazement, excitement even, of what had happened to us was wearing off. We were now realizing that this wasn't a dream or a joke. It was a frightening reality and we were probably in a lot of trouble. On top of that, we were exhausted. Rory was so tired that his little legs could hardly keep him going. The last thing I needed was even more complaining from Olive Ayres.

"Oh Olive, just shut up," I told her. I expected her to start arguing with me. Instead I heard her say:

"Uh-oh." She was higher up than the rest of us, so she could see a little further up the road.

"'Uh-oh' what?" I asked, against my better judgment. Whatever she had seen, it was not going to be good for us.

"We're not going to that Timaru place," she told us. "We're going right to Scary Forest." Her voice trembled. She held out her arm to point and that was trembling too.

We all stopped walking, except for Clyde who didn't get the message. Poor Olive was stuck on his back plodding closer and closer to the sinisterly-named Scary Forest.

"Stop," we heard her telling him as he continued on his way. "Stop, stop, whoa; hey horse, I'm talking to you," she continued, her voice fading as she was taken further and further away.

To be honest, it was a relief to have Olive out of earshot for a few minutes. The three of us crowded together to discuss our plans.

"We can't really go back," I pointed out. "There's nothing behind us except fields of pumpkins and goats. We'll have to carry on."

"But I don't want to go to Scary Forest," Rory wailed, sounding like a two-year-old who wasn't allowed ice cream. He sat down right in the middle of the roadway, crossed his arms, and put on his grumpiest and most stubborn expression.

I sighed. This was his favorite trick in the mall to try and make Dad buy him whatever it was he wanted. So, just like Dad always did, we ignored him.

"I say we go on," agreed Persis. She glanced at her precious axe. "If there are trees, I might need to chop some wood to make a fire. Then we could keep warm, and if we found some food, we could cook it."

It sounded sensible; but really, she just wanted to play with her axe—I could tell.

"Clyde!" I yelled. Clyde was now so far into the distance that he looked the size of a small pony. He had to perform an elaborate turn in the narrow road: shuffling forward, and then backward, and then forward, to be able to turn around. He trotted back, and dropped his head to nibble at a very lush-looking clump of grass.

Olive slithered right along his neck, did a roly-poly over his head, and landed on her feet, looking surprised.

"Rory," I said, in my bossiest voice, "Rory, you are going to ride on Clyde." Then I turned to Olive. "Uh-uh," I interrupted, holding up my hand to stop her saying anything, and wagging my finger. "Olive, you can make some shoes out of leaves and tie them around your feet until we find something better."

It felt like everyone kept expecting me to tell them what to do, so just this once, I had decided to do it. Nothing with these three happened quickly though. It took five minutes to persuade Rory to get over his tantrum and get up and then another five minutes to push and pull him onto Clyde's back. After that it took ten more minutes for Olive to find leaves of a shade of green that she liked and which could be tied around her feet and ankles with the runner from a pumpkin in a nearby field. And another five minutes were spent on getting Clyde to stop eating and turn back around.

Eventually we were heading the right way, and what's more, it smelled delicious. As we drew nearer to the edge of the woods, we all lifted our noses to the air and sniffed.

"Cinnamon," I breathed.

"Peppermint," Rory and Persis chorused.

"Chocolate!" shrieked Olive, with drool running down her chin.

CHAPTER 13

The wonderful smells twitched at our noses and dragged us along the roadway ever closer to Scary Forest. Our stomachs rumbled and gurgled with the hope of food. Anything that smelled so amazing must taste wonderful—or so our stomachs believed. We were no longer afraid or tired. We were just ravenous.

As we hurried along, we hardly noticed what was happening around us. At first, there was just a scattering of trees. They looked like normal trees at first: smooth bark, pretty green leaves and straight branches. A few paces in, though, the trees became more menacing. They grew closer together and their branches meshed overhead to become a canopy. Their bark was gnarled and dark, with pits and holes that almost looked like faces. The branches were crooked and the twigs reached out to snag our clothes and hair when we wandered too close.

Soon the failing sunlight could scarcely break through the dark leaves and we slowed our pace a little. We fell silent. We could hear little rustling sounds in the branches and on the ground.

"Animals," said Olive, anxiously peering into the undergrowth.

"Snakes and spiders," said Rory, enthusiastically.

"Wolves," muttered Persis hopefully.

"Dragons," added Rory, wildly. We all bunched together as close as we could and walked slowly.

Rumble, rumble said our stomachs.

By now, the smell of home-baking, warm cookies and toasted buns dripping with butter was making us all feel ill with hunger. As we had been walking along, the roadway had narrowed until it was a footpath and we had to walk single file.

Persis, who was at the front, suddenly stopped, and we all bumped into her one after the other.

"What did you stop for?" I asked, standing on tiptoes to peer over her shoulder.

"Oh my," breathed Olive as she peered over the other shoulder. We must have looked like a strange three-headed monster, but we didn't care. We had seen something. Ahead of us was a house. And I think you can probably guess exactly what kind of house would be in a clearing in a spooky forest, considering the types of aromas we had been inhaling.

It was an honest-to-goodness gingerbread cottage. It stood in a clearing near a fountain that gurgled a rich, brown liquid. Steam rose gently from it. It was a chocolate fountain; I could smell the warm chocolate from where I stood. It was surrounded by little pink shrubs made from cotton candy. The cottage itself was huge with icing around the windows and big peppermint lollipops planted in the flower beds. Swirling patterns made of different types of candy were embedded in the gingerbread walls. The smell of warm baked goods was making me dizzy with hunger, but I was wary.

"I think we should be careful," I began. "We know that wicked witches always live in gingerbread cottages—it's in all the stories." But I had wasted my breath. Before I had finished my sentence, Rory had slid down from Clyde and along with Persis and Olive, he was scooping up crumbs from the ground and shoveling them into mouth. Clyde nudged me out of the way, sending me flying off the path, and moseyed over to join them. He had spotted some taffy apples that lay cooling on a table nearby. He crunched them up, sticks and all.

Olive had stood up and was licking a window.

"Ith's thugar!" she exclaimed. "Thugar that's been thpun tho thinly that it'th clear," she marveled, with her tongue still stuck to the pane.

Now Rory had snapped off a lump of window sill decorated with swags of white icing sugar, and was devouring it.

"Mmmm, gingerbread," he drooled.

Persis had found that the door handle was made of chocolate and had broken it right off. She held it with both hands and crammed it into her mouth.

"Um, guys?" I tried to get their attention. What if someone was inside the house watching Olive lick their window from the other side? They carried on eating. "Guys?" I tried again.

By now, Persis had realized that the "welcome" mat was made of fudge and had ripped off a fistful of it. Rory and Olive had hurried to join her and were soon on their hands and knees like animals.

I glanced around the clearing but saw nothing and no one. There were still the noises of small animals moving in the undergrowth but nothing that sounded like a wicked witch, or her minions, coming to get us.

Not that I knew what that sounded like, of course.

Oh well, if you can't beat them, join them, I thought. So I did just that. I pulled up a small bush that looked like a lollipop. It tasted just like an orange, peppermint, pineapple, and chocolate lollipop. All my favorite flavors combined. I started to lick daintily, but ended up chomping and crunching.

"Brina, get a hold of yourself. You need to stop eating this person's house," I told myself.

Twenty minutes later, I managed to control myself and I stopped. Wow. I had worked through most of the flower bed and the others had taken out the front door, the window sills, and one entire window—and had even nibbled away at most of the cottage's foundations.

I started to feel guilty. This was someone's home, after all.

"Hey, you guys. I feel bad about this," I called out.

"Yeah, I feel pretty sick, too," complained Persis, holding her swollen stomach.

"No, I mean we just ate someone's house," I explained. "We should probably leave a note or something. Say we're sorry and we'll somehow make it right when we can."

The others looked at me, then at each other. They looked down and shuffled their feet, and put their hands behind their backs.

"Got a pen?" asked Persis.

"Of course not," I said. "But there must be something inside the house."

No one moved, which was no surprise. They always seemed to wait for me to do things or come up with ideas. It was starting to get on my nerves.

As I started to walk toward the gap where the front door had been, I noticed a sign on the wall; it was made from smooth dark chocolate with white chocolate writing. It looked like the kind of sign you might see outside a dentist, but there would be worse terrors for anyone visiting this place. I had been right all along.

Ms. Witchy Wu
Tasty Children Welcome

Tasty children welcome? Tasty? I bet they were—for her lunch! It was time to run.

CHAPTER 14

I pointed at the sign; my sticky fingers were shaking. Persis and Olive both took a step backward. I could tell they were thinking the same as me. Rory frowned and screwed up his eyes. He didn't like the curls and swirls in the writing. I could almost see the words dancing in front of his eyes from the way he held his hand up to try and slow them down, so I read it out to him.

"It says we're welcome," he said. Seriously, how could someone as naughty as my little brother still be so innocent?

"It means that children are welcome to be her supper," I explained but the space where Rory had been a second ago was empty. He had sprinted to the far side of the clearing where the trees began again, with Olive and Persis panting right behind him.

Huh, thanks for waiting for me. Clyde and I hurried over to join them and we hid behind some bushes. For some reason, Clyde seemed to be looking up at the sky as he trotted along. I glanced up but could only see the evening's first stars coming out. Then I saw a patch of darkness swoop in front of the stars, blocking their light. It began to descend, closer and closer to the gingerbread cottage. That was no cloud.

"Guys, I think we need to get out of here," I began. Then my blood turned to ice in my veins. From just above us a terrible screech split the twilight.

"Aaaarrrrrrrrgggg! My house; my precious house!"

The sound was so shrill and loud that Clyde whinnied, reared up, and broke wind in fright. And then I spoke some words that I had never thought I would ever say, let alone believe.

"I think the witch is home," I whispered. We all shrank back further into the trees as quietly as we could. The branches hid us, but also stopped us from seeing what was happening. Hearing was what was going on was plenty, though.

"My door knob," the voice screamed. Then, "My door!"

Uh-oh, we were in big trouble. I could hear footsteps as what must be the Witchy Wu whose name was on the sign ran around her property, wailing at the destruction we had caused. We needed to get away and we needed to do it fast. I looked at Clyde. He was huge and he had fantastic stamina and speed. If we all got on him, just for a little while, he would be able to get us away. I whispered my plan to the others, and Clyde bent his face down among us, just as if he was listening in. After all we had experienced in the past few hours, I wouldn't have been at all surprised to find out that a Clydesdale unicorn understood human language.

I started with Rory, and put my arms around his ribs. He giggled and told me to stop tickling him. Honestly! I ignored him and hefted him onto Clyde's back then turned to Olive and Persis. As I started to bend down so that they could climb onto Clyde, using me as a stool, we heard running footsteps and the sound of branches and shrubs being trampled.

She was heading straight for us.

"I'm coming to get you, you wicked, greedy little monsters!" the witch howled. Clyde reared again, but this time he bolted, and headed for the footpath, which glimmered in the twilight. I wanted to yell, "Not that way!" I was certain that this Witchy Wu person would be on the path as well, but there was no way Clyde was stopping. All I could do was stare in horror as Rory was bounced around on his back like a rag doll. Instinctively, I started to follow, but Olive grabbed a handful of my hair and yanked hard.

"Get down," she hissed, and shoved me to the ground. Persis dove down next to us, crushing me beneath her. The last thing we saw was Rory being bounced so high that he flew into the air and caught hold of Clyde's horn on the way down. He wrapped his legs and arms around it and dangled underneath, blocking Clyde's view as he galloped deeper into Scary Forest.

I tried to get up again, but the others pulled me back down. In the case of Olive, she pulled me down painfully hard, but they were right. A shadow darker than midnight hurtled past us, just a few feet away— Witchy Wu was heading in the direction Rory and Clyde had gone. Icy terror trickled through our veins. Even if I had wanted to get to my feet and run after them, I was so paralyzed with fear that I couldn't have moved if I had tried.

As we lay there, the shadow passed us again; the witch was returning to the gingerbread cottage —sorry, gingerbread ruin. When she had gone, feeling returned to our arms and legs and we staggered to our feet.

"Come on," I said, fighting the tears that were threatening to make me seem not cool. "We have to get after them." We started off, following the direction of the pathway and hopefully the way that Clyde and Rory had been going. I could hardly breath I was so scared that something had happened to Rory. I picked up my pace and began to run. Then one of the trees I was passing reached out and grabbed hold of my dress with its branch.

CHAPTER 15

I yanked at the fabric, and heard a rip, but I was past caring and hurried on. Behind me I heard Olive give a little yelp of pain.

"Hey, Brina, wait a minute," Persis hissed. I paused and looked back. Olive was caught up by her dress and hair, and even her skin, by a vicious-looking thorn bush. As she pulled away, I saw specks of blood appear on her arms where the thorns had dragged across her. I blinked and looked again, harder. It seemed as though the branches on the bush had deliberately tightened on Olive to make it as difficult and painful as possible to free herself. I could see the same puzzled expression on Persis' face as must have been on mine. Had the thorn bush moved by itself? Had that tree deliberately reached out one of its branches to try to snag me?

I shook my head.

No.

No way. Trees didn't move, not even in somewhere as strange as Dralfynia.

"Are you okay?" Persis asked Olive. She nodded, sucking at the bubbles of blood on her wrist.

"Come on," I said, my mind on Rory. "We need to get out of here." I turned, took one step and immediately fell to my knees. A root that I could have sworn hadn't been there a moment before, seemed to tangle around my knees, and I stumbled, face first, into a pile of leaves.

Yuk. Old leaves taste and smell gross. One went in my mouth, and I spat it out as I sat up.

"Did you see that?" Persis asked Olive, her eyes round. Olive nodded.

"Sure did. That root tripped Sabrina up on purpose." It sounded ridiculous but when I got to my feet, her face was serious.

"I think that these trees and bushes are trying to trap us," Olive said. They were certainly trying to hurt us—and they were succeeding. But trap us?

"Why?" I asked. She looked at me as though I wasn't thinking straight.

"So that the witch can come get us," she explained. Oh. Unfortunately, that made a lot of sense.

"Look, guys, we need to get to Rory and Clyde, right?" Persis said. She had taken out her little hatchet and she was gripping its wooden handle with both hands. "So, we're going to need to get away." Her face was grim and her eyes flashed in the gloom. She had completely taken command. "I'm going to lead the way, and anything that gets in my way gets a taste of my axe." She raised her voice and it rang out clear and strong. Then she spoke more quietly. "You two stick close behind me. Don't even think about leaving the trail that I'm going to make. Okay?"

Olive and I nodded. I had never seen Persis so deadly serious, and somehow it made me even more frightened than I already was. She turned away, whirled the axe in circles above her head, and brought it down with a terrific smash on the root that had tripped me. It split in two, and the tree that it belonged to shrank back.

"Follow me!" Persis yelled, brandishing the axe wildly and leaping over the remains of the root.

"Persis, Persis," I called after her. "Rory and Clyde went that way," I told her, pointing to the left. She didn't miss a beat. She swerved, changed direction and charged off, swinging the axe at any twig, root, or branch that came near her. As Olive and I followed behind her, we could see the trees move out of her way. But worse, we could now make out the gnarls in the bark. They looked like eyes and mouths, and they looked full of rage.

CHAPTER 16

At first, we made good progress, but eventually poor Persis began to tire. Every branch that reached for us fell victim to her sharp blade, but the violent shudders it sent up her arms when the axe fell were exhausting her. Her face was flushed and sweat poured from her. She was starting to slow down. I tried to take the axe from her.

"Let's take it in turns," I said. She shook her head "It won't work, Brina. You're Rapunzel. You're a princess. It's me that has to do this. I'm the one who's the woodcutter's daughter." It sounded ridiculous, but in Dralfynia, it was the kind of logic that made sense. So Olive and I huddled behind Persis as she chopped and hacked. Every time a tree grabbed my hair with its hand-like twigs, Persis rescued me by splitting the tree's branch in half. She was staggering with fatigue by the time that I caught a glimpse of yellow ahead of us.

"The path!" I screamed. "Just there. The path! It's too wide for the trees to get us."

My words gave Persis the final burst of energy that she needed. She surged forward, burst out from between two shrubs, and collapsed in the center of the path.

Olive and I huddled over her.

"Whoa, you were amazing," I told her.

She managed a feeble smile.

"Yeah, I totally was, wasn't I?"

I gave her a few minutes to recover and helped her cool down by fanning her with some of my hair. Olive had taken the hatchet and stood on guard, watching for anything that might move from the leafy forest floor to the hard, gritty path. She brandished it at one tree that moved its roots onto the crushed stone and I saw it flinch and pull back.

"Guys," she said, "I think we're safe as long as we stay on the path. The trees don't seem to like how the stones feel." This was good to know, especially as we had to keep going. It had become darker and colder, and we still had to find Rory and Clyde. I held out an arm and Persis used it to pull herself up.

"We need to keep going. I'm so sorry, you must be pooped," I said.

She nodded. "I'll be okay," she began, but was interrupted by a loud rattling of dry branches and leaves; that sound was then sliced by a scream.

It was Rory's voice and he sounded terrified. We began to run, bumping into each other and pushing one another out of the way in sheer panic. I could hear crashing sounds and more shrieking and yelling. I increased my pace.

After five hard minutes, sprinting became painful. My lungs were burning and my legs quivered with fatigue. Persis and Olive couldn't keep up and fell behind. I was running so fast I got a stitch in my side and wanted to be sick—the sweets and gingerbread were sloshing around in my stomach as if they wanted to come back up again. I didn't realize it, but I was crying. Tears were flying from my eyes as I ran.

Up ahead, I saw a terrible sight. Clyde was standing by a huge tree, and caught up in its branches, high up in the air, was my little brother. Rory screamed and writhed and wriggled, his face crimson. I ran to the tree and began to thump its broad trunk, shrieking at it to let go of him.

Persis and Olive caught up with me, and Persis raised her axe once more, bringing it down with a great, juddering blow, and embedding it deep into the bark. The tree flung its branches upward and Rory fell downward, landing on his back in a pile of ferns and moss.

He sprang to his feet and glared at me.

"Hey, leave Russell alone!" he yelled. His fists were on his hips and his chin was jutting out.

"Are you okay?" I asked, as I bent to check him over.

He shoved me aside.

"Of course I'm OK," he said crossly. "Are you okay, Russell?" He turned his back on me and looked at the tree. It was huge. It was easily the largest we had seen in the whole of Scary Forest. It shook its leaves and twisted its trunk so that the knots in its bark became cross-eyed, looking down at the axe which was buried where its nose would be. Rory strode across and tried to pull it out.

"Ouch that hurts," a deep, growly voice rumbled. Persis stepped up and flicked the axe out.

"I guess you have to do it fast, like pulling off a band-aid," she commented. She was taking this way better than me.

"I don't understand what's going on. Wasn't that tree attacking you?" I demanded.

"Not all trees in Scary Forest are under the control of Witchy Wu," Russell growled. "For some of us, our bark is worse than our bite." Oh great. A talking tree that liked puns.

"So why were you screaming?" I asked Rory.

He started to giggle again with the memory.

"Russell was tickling me," he said. "He's great, isn't he?" he added, staring adoringly at the tree. "He wants to branch out into stand-up comedy."

Russell made a strange noise that could have been laughter. A laughing tree? Could this day get any weirder? I wondered.

Then Olive joined in.

"Oh, I think I've twigged now. Russell's a good tree, but we should leaf those other trees alone?"

"Yeah, that wood be a good idea," added Persis.

Really? Was I the only person with even a little common sense? I sighed. I just wanted all this to be over.

"So what happened to you?" I asked.

"Russell saved my life," Rory replied.

CHAPTER 17

"After you threw me onto Clyde's back," Rory began, giving me a glare. Honestly, he is so irritating.

"I 'threw' you there to save your butt from that witch," I reminded him. After all, a little gratitude now and then would be nice.

He ignored me.

"Well, I got bounced up and landed on Clyde's horn—and I just had to hang there while he galloped along. It was pretty scary, to be honest."

I imagined it had been. Rory must have been gripping onto that slippery unicorn horn knowing that if he fell, he'd be trampled underneath Clyde's hooves. It sent shivers up my spine as I listened to him.

"And then we came to a big, um, crack in the earth," he said.

"You mean like a valley or a ravine?" I asked.

He nodded.

"Yeah. So then Clyde stopped really fast," he said, giving Clyde a reproving look.

Clyde bent his head, looking for all the world like a very embarrassed unicorn. He munched some rotten apples and dry acorns that were lying on the ground, and his stomach rumbled.

"But then I lost my grip on his horn," Rory continued, "and I went flying into the air— right over the valley thing, and over all these really sharp rocks—and Russell put out his branches to catch me. And now we're best friends," Rory concluded, looking surprisingly chipper for someone who had just escaped death.

I owed Russell a big 'thank you' for saving my brother, so I said it in a way I thought he would appreciate.

"It's knot that I didn't trust yew," I began. "I guess I couldn't cedar forest for the trees. We weren't expecting to meet a talking tree. I know Rory will pine for you, and thanks fir saving him. I willow you one for that."

Hey, if you can't beat them, join them. Rory gave Russell a hug and we turned to leave, following the direction Russell's branches pointed us in.

We made our way back to the path, leaving behind a gigantic, chuckling oak tree. I told Persis to get on Clyde's back for a break, and we kept close together, afraid to get within reach of any vines or grasping twigs.

So here we were again. Walking, walking and more walking. But at least we were safe from the witch whose home we'd eaten. I said as much out loud to try and cheer everyone up. I spoke too soon, of course, but I had yet to learn that every time I felt safe in Dralfynia was when I should really start to worry.

"So about that witch lady?" Rory asked.

"Yeah, what about her?"

"She said she wanted to eat us," said Rory; I could tell he was impressed in spite of his fright. "Do you think she meant all of us and Clyde as well? She must have a big appetite." Persis laughed.

"She'll never be able to catch us if that's her average meal then," she kidded.

"Did you hear her name?" added Olive. "Witchy Wu?" She started to giggle. "Who is this Witchy Wu? I mean, Wu who?"

Clyde joined in the hilarity by breaking wind for five seconds flat. We all burst into peals of laughter, so that we were bent over double and hardly able to talk. Some of it was shock; some of it was Clyde's robust fart. But when the smell hit us, we stopped.

"Those taffy apples were a mistake," I said. "Not to mention the acorns and rotten apples when we were with Russell."

Clyde swung his kind, intelligent face around to look at me with reproach in his eyes.

"Sorry, big fellow," I said standing up and nuzzling his head with mine. I think we all felt safer knowing he was with us. In fact, it was his special talent that saved us right there and then.

"What's that buzzing noise?" Olive wanted to know.

At exactly the same time, Persis asked, "Why is it getting so dark all of a sudden?"

A thrumming drone filled the air and the evening sky grew darker. Winding through the canopy of trees, a dark cloud headed right for us—a cloud that boiled and bubbled and vibrated with electricity.

"It's the witch," Olive guessed. "She's sent something to get us." We turned and started to hurry along the path to get away, but the cloud was too fast. As it came closer, we saw it wasn't simply a cloud: it was a dense swarm of bats. Flying in tight formation, their black bodies blocked the light, but their sharp teeth, bright eyes, and jagged claws glittered. The sound we could hear was the frantic beating of their leathery wings in the still air. The first bat swooped down to snatch at my long hair and, screaming wildly, I waved my arms and managed to smack it away. It gave a high-pitched squeal and flew up to join its buddies.

As we cowered on the ground, the shapeless cloud was reforming, drawing tighter and sharper. The bats were working together to form an arrow shape, and it was pointing right at us.

CHAPTER 18

The lead bat swooped low and stretched its claws wide, reaching for my face. I whirled away and tried to drop to the ground but it snagged my hair. Screaming, I fell to my knees and tried swat the bat with my hands, but it was joined by another, then another. Their claws were so long and sharp that I felt them sinking into my scalp, and knew they had drawn blood. Even so, they sliced through my skin so neatly that it took me a few seconds to register the searing pain.

Olive and Rory screamed, and I blinked trickles of blood from my eyes to look for them. In their panic they had left the safety of the path and run back into the forest. Then they vanished from my sight, hiding behind a thick bush with glossy, dark leaves.

I heard Persis yell and saw her slide from Clyde's back, pulling up her red riding hood to protect her head. She fumbled around until she found her axe, which she had tucked into her frilly, white apron. She hauled it out and, ignoring her aching shoulders and arms, she whirled it around and around. She caught one bat hard and sent it tumbling to the ground. I had managed to rip two bats from my hair and they were now on my hands, like mittens. As I watched, one opened its mouth to reveal pointed teeth. I shrieked and flapped my arms round, dislodging the bats and flinging them as far from me as I could. My heart thudded as I tucked my hands around my waist and bent to protect them. I could see the terrified gazes of Rory and Olive as the bush they had hidden behind gathered up its branches like a long skirt, stood up, and walked away, exposing them to the bat attack again.

Clyde gave out an almighty, very smelly fart.

The bats zoomed low and then, inexplicably, zoomed back upward and over our heads. I thought they were toying with us as they circled overhead like vultures waiting to attack once more.

Clyde farted again. This one was his best effort so far. We all felt a gentle brush of warm air, and the stench filled our nostrils. Olive—who, as we already knew, had a weak stomach—started to gag.

The bats circled higher, away from Clyde and Persis, but several broke formation to attack Rory, Olive and me again.

"Come here!" Persis yelled to us. "They don't like Clyde's farts!" she shouted. I could see that she was right. I ran over and stood close to Clyde, holding my nose and trying to breathe through my mouth. That didn't help much, as I could still taste the smell of the rotting-apple fart on my tongue. I tried not to think about it and reached out, grabbed Rory, and pulled him close to me.

Olive was on her hands and knees at the edge of the path. Her body was convulsing as she dry-retched. She couldn't even stand up. Telling Rory to stay right where he was and hold his nose, I bent low and scooted over to her. Persis gave me some cover from the bats with her swirling axe, and I pulled Olive to her feet and hauled her along with me, ignoring her as she coughed and dribbled and heaved.

We huddled into Clyde and covered our faces as best we could. Clyde lowered his head, steadied his strong legs and broke wind again and again. I stared upward in disbelief. The cloud of bats began to disintegrate as they flew in different directions. Some flew into other bats; some flew into trees and were briefly stunned. They began to flit away in the direction of the gingerbread cottage, flying faster and more steadily the further away they got from the toxic-fart zone.

CHAPTER 19

Gray sky showed through the leaves again.

The bats had gone. Clyde had stopped farting and a gentle breeze blew the remaining smell away. We patted Clyde, congratulating him and making a great fuss of him. "I think that his, um, emissions, affected the bats by disrupting their magnetic compasses," Olive told us.

Annoying and mean and whiney though she is, Olive is still one of the cleverest kids in our school.

"It's what they use to navigate; without that, they couldn't tell where they were so they flew away," she explained.

Clyde gave a tiny parp of happiness. His work now was done.

So, now what? Rory, Olive and Persis all looked at me. I rolled my eyes and thought about how nice it would be if someone else made a decision—just once.

Olive must have read my mind. She spoke up.

"I think we should keep going along the path through the woods," she said. "It must come to an end eventually, and we can't go back that way," she added, pointing toward the gingerbread cottage and the direction in which the bats had flown.

When I had wished that someone else would make a decision, I hadn't meant her! But she was right; there was nothing else for it.

"I agree," I said. "Well done, Olive," I added, a little ashamed that I had been jealous.

We began walking again. Persis lead the way alongside Clyde. They were followed by Olive, then me, then Rory. It was starting to get really dark, and the trees seemed to be thicker. We could hardly see where to put our feet, even though the crushed stones that made up the path gave off a very faint, white light.

We were a little jumpy after the encounter with the trees that could move and then the witch's troop of trained bats. Every rustling leaf and groaning branch made one of us jump, which made the rest of us jump. Once I felt something tickle the back of my neck and I almost leapt out of my skin, but it was just a cobweb that I had brushed past.

We continued on our way. We were too tired and unsettled to speak. We just wanted to be out of this horrible forest and back in fresh air again. We focused on putting one foot in front of the other again and again until we thought we couldn't manage one more step.

"Hey guys, I think we're nearly there," Persis called from up ahead. "The trees are thinning out." She passed the message to Olive, who passed it onto me. I turned my head to pass it back to Rory.

But Rory was no longer behind me.

My first thought was that he'd better not be messing around or he'd be in trouble with me. Then the raw fear swept over me, paralyzing my limbs and choking my voice in my throat. There could be only one reason. He had been the last in line, and the witch had obviously crept up after us and taken him.

I managed to force out a little croak, and Olive and Persis realized something was wrong. They hurried back to me with worry in their eyes. Then they saw I was alone, and panic replaced the worry.

"RORY!" screamed Persis as loudly as she could. At first all we heard was more rustling. Was that him? Was it someone—or something— taking Rory away?

We all yelled his name together, even Clyde whinnied along with us. All we heard was the sound of rustling in the undergrowth. Then came the sound of Rory's young voice laughing and laughing. Oh boy, he was off with Russell again.

"You sawdust on them," he gasped out; he was giggling too hard to talk properly. "Thanks Russell," he said, in a calmer voice.

"Welcome," rumbled the familiar tree-like voice, which appeared to come from the very center of Russell's trunk.

"So when the path forks we go right?" Rory was asking him.

The leaves rustled again, which I assumed was the tree equivalent of nodding.

When Rory and Russell came into view I glared at them.

"You have to quit running off like that," I said through teeth that were clenched so tight my jaw ached. "We thought something bad had happened to you again." Rory took one look at my furious, frightened face and dipped his head.

"Sorry," he muttered. "I just noticed Russell following us and asked him for a lift. My legs were tired."

"All our legs are tired," I pointed out. "Just say something, next time, okay?"

Rory nodded, but he always does that. It looks like he cares about being yelled at, but he takes no notice at all.

I sighed. I had more important things to worry about.

"We need to get out of here and find some shelter. It's getting cold." I shivered as I spoke. It was night now, and the temperature had dropped.

Rory raised his hand and waved 'goodbye' to his new best friend and walked over to me.

"Russell says we take the right-hand path when the road splits when we come to it," he told me. "He's pretty cool, isn't he? Did you know he's 253 years old? He can walk, though not very fast, and he hates that witch who chased us. And he's got a secret crush on an elm tree but he's too shy to tell her."

I led the way back to Clyde, shaking my head to myself. A lovesick talking tree called Russell was my brother's best friend.

This particular lovesick talking tree was right, though. We soon found a fork in the path, turned right and followed Clyde along the track for only another fifteen minutes before we were out of the forest at last. I turned my face up to the moon and breathed in deeply. Open space at last, and the smell of decaying leaves was gone. Bliss.

We were surrounded by … guess what? More fields, just like the ones on the other side of the woods. In spite of the full moon riding high in the sky, it was still extremely dark. There was no way we could continue until morning. We had to bed down for the night.

Clyde solved the problem for us. He had turned from the path and walked into a field with heaped haystacks dotted across the ground. He stopped by the first one and stood there, looking at us.

"I think he wants us to sleep there, in that haystack," said Rory, who was enjoying his new position as best buddy to all magical creatures. I pinched my lower lip and thought about it. It would be cozy, and we would be camouflaged from any bats flying overhead. I gave a little nod. It was a pretty good idea. We became little bunny rabbits and burrowed deep into the pile of hay, sniffing its warm scent. One by one—and before I could manage to suggest that we take it in turns to keep guard—we fell deeply asleep.

CHAPTER 20

We woke up the next morning to find a unicorn eating our bed.

"Clyde," I said crossly, "we were fast asleep. And that's like eating our house, by the way." I climbed out of the haystack and gingerly touched my scalp. Luckily the wounds left by the bats seemed to be healing.

Persis scrambled out on her hands and knees and stood up with an enormous yawn. She scratched her belly and picked some straw from her braids.

"Well, it's probably only fair, really, seeing as we ate Witchy Wu's gingerbread cottage," she pointed out reasonably enough. "You know, what goes around comes around," she said.

Rory rolled out of the haystack and stared at her. This was a new concept for him.

"So if you're mean to someone then someone else will be mean to you later on," she explained.

Rory nodded, though he looked a little worried.

"I know what you mean," he told her. "One time Bridget wouldn't let me have a sleepover on a school night, which I decided was mean of her, so I put a fake spider in her slippers, which in return was mean of me. She screamed the house down," he finished, with a satisfied smile.

Persis opened her mouth to explain that wasn't quite what she meant, but she closed it again and shook her head instead.

Well, Rory might not have understood the idea of being nice to people so that they will be nice to you, but he had reminded us why we were even here at all.

Bridget. Where had she vanished to? She must have seen us all laying on the ground when she landed in Dralfynia, and had just gone off and left us.

"We need to find Bridget," I said. I looked over at Clyde. "Do you know where she is?" I asked him. I was tired of all this pointless wandering around. Also, I was hungry again, I had half a haystack stuck in my annoying hair, and I really just wanted to go home.

Clyde dipped his head once.

Olive came up to me. She looked even worse than she had yesterday. Straw peeked out of her dress, her leaf shoes had disintegrated, and she was even dirtier than before.

"I think he said 'yes'," she declared. I supposed she was doing her best to fit in with the rest of us. After all, she hadn't complained for ages. She pushed forward to talk to Clyde.

"Clyde, can you lead us to where she is?" she demanded. Another dip of the head.

"How far away is it?" I tried.

Nothing.

Then Olive realized something.

"He can only answer yes or no, like that game from elementary school," Olive explained. "Clyde, if we carry on walking, will we get there today?"

He nodded again.

She pointed up the path away from Scary Forest. "Is it that way?" she asked, getting excited.

He nodded.

"Fantastic." She rubbed her hands together, which sent clouds of black grime into the air, but I shared her enthusiasm.

"C'mon troops," I called out. "Let's hit the road again. Clyde says Bridget went that way and it's not too far."

In a few minutes, we were assembled and marching along, leaving bits of hay in our wake, like Hansel and Gretel leaving a trail. Magpies and sparrows swooped down after us to collect it for their nests.

Behind us, Clyde nodded his head again, and then he shook it. A piece of straw was caught in his mane and it was irritating him. After shaking his head vigorously, he finally dislodged it.

CHAPTER 21

So we did a bit more of what we were getting pretty good at. We walked. Olive had created a new pair of leaf shoes—she was practically an expert at making them now. This pair had laces that went up her ankles. I was sure that the next pair would have heels.

We began to see signs that human beings lived nearby. The fields became smaller and were neat shapes with smart wooden fences instead of scattered heaps of stones. There were gates, too, some roped shut. The track we followed became wider and smoother, and we spotted plumes of smoke in the far distance.

Smoke meant that there were welcoming fires in warm houses, freshly baked bread, comfortable chairs, and places to wash. We were all desperate to brush our teeth, as apparently our mouths felt and smelt as if small rodents had crawled in there to die. You can thank Rory for that charming image, of course. He told me that was how my breath smelled when I leaned close to him to ask him if he was okay.

Soon, we could even pick up the scent of wood smoke. Without any need for discussion, we increased our pace until we were hurrying along. After another bit of walking, we saw some low, stone buildings with thatched roofs in the hazy distance. As we got closer, we noticed that some of the other buildings were wooden with pointed roofs and ornate paintings around their arched windows.

Then we saw people.

Real, ordinary, human people. Admittedly they were dressed in weird old-fashioned clothes like ours, but we could hear them now, and they were talking English.

"Hey, Jack," called out one man, who was leading an ox cart piled high with pumpkins. "Don't forget to feed the pigs."

"Okay, Uncle Jack, I will," a younger guy replied, as he hurried past with a bucket full of carrot tops and potato peelings.

My stomach growled.

"Why isn't anyone looking at us?" Olive wondered. "I mean, we look pretty strange," she said, gesturing at Rory in particular.

I thought about it.

"Well, I assume it's because we don't look strange for here, just for twenty-first century Melas." My stomach growled again, louder this time. I looked around to see if I could find somewhere that might give us food, but Persis was way ahead of me.

"Look, an inn," she said. "We can just check in there."

"An in what?" Rory was puzzled.

"No doofus, I mean an inn. It's kind of like a café with rooms above where you can sleep. We stayed in one when we went to Vermont last fall. It was awesome. I even had a four-poster bed."

Food, beds, and presumably showers. It sounded like just the place for us.

Unfortunately, we had one problem.

"I hate to be the one to pour cold water on your so-called ideas," sniped Olive, "but we have no money."

She was right. We straggled to a stop and wondered what to do.

"Luckily for you losers, I have a plan," she said, with a smirk, and strode over to the dingy building. The inn had walls made from thick stone, with tiny holes cut into them to allow light in and smoke out. It looked a bit grubby and weeds grew outside in amongst the vegetables and flowers that surrounded it.

A wooden sign swung from a pole outside the door. It read: 'The Inn of the Fluffy Kitten,' in swirly writing. The sign was made from wooden planks nailed together and on it someone had painted an image of a very fluffy kitten. The kitten was gray with a white tip on its tail, and it had orange eyes. Surely with a name like that the inn had to be safe? Olive opened the door and we began to follow her. As I passed beneath the sign, I thought I heard a tiny 'meow' and I looked up. Either my eyes were playing tricks on me or the kitten had changed position. I squinted at it, but I saw nothing and I turned away. I heard another 'meow' and whirled back. The kitten had definitely moved. Now it sat with its back to me. I stared again for a long minute before deciding that the kitten had been teasing me and was now bored with the game. I followed Olive and the others inside—and immediately wished I hadn't.

It reeked of smelly clothes; the floor was gritty underfoot, and all the furniture—rough wooden benches, rickety tables, and a long serving-bar—was covered in sticky stuff that I didn't want to know about.

"Excuse me," Olive called out. You could just tell she was used to giving orders and having them obeyed. "Excuse me, who is in charge here?" Three exceedingly hairy, short men, who were clutching metal mugs in their hands, turned to stare at her, then turned away.

A head popped up from behind the serving bar. It was a boy, perhaps fourteen years old, with straw-colored hair, cute dimples and clear blue eyes.

He met Olive's gaze.

"I'm in charge," he said.

"Well, my man. My friends and I need a room, stabling for our unicorn, and refreshments. And we don't have any money."

CHAPTER 22

That was her plan? Just to tell the truth? Rory, Persis and I shuffled back a few steps and casually glanced up at the ceiling or down at the floor. Perhaps they wouldn't think we were with her. Plus, I was a little irked that she had called me her friend. At best, we were frenemies.

The boy didn't look pleased at being called "my man". He gave Olive a very cool, appraising look, which took in her grimy skin, her ragged clothes and her unkempt hair.

"You can work for your keep if you like," he told her. "Can you clean?"

"Oh gosh yes, I love cleaning," Olive squealed with excitement. Then she clapped her hand over her mouth in shock. I think her Dralfynia Cinderella character was taking over, because I was pretty sure that in our world, Olive didn't like cleaning at all. Nonetheless, the boy handed her a rag and a wooden pail of cold water. She looked at it with disgust.

"Oh no," Olive exclaimed. "This won't do at all. I need hot water, some soap and a clean rag. Not this!" She threw the rag on the fire in the corner of the room, ripped one of her many patches from the skirt of her dress, revealing a new patch of a different pattern beneath it, and then tipped the cold water into a great black pot that hung on a pole above the fire to heat it up.

She looked happier than I had ever seen her and at last the clothes we wore had some use. I guess they only disintegrated when we tried to throw them away. She even began to hum. Within a few minutes, she had hot soapy water and was sloshing it on every surface in the room.

The three hairy men muttered in disgust and slipped out of the room, collecting sacks and pickaxes on their way out. As they passed us, they stared hard at both Rory and me.

Rory, Persis and I sat down at a table that was soaking wet and covered in suds. Olive ripped off another patch and swooped down on us, drying the table. Now she was singing out loud.

I caught the boy's eye and he came over to join us. I wanted to ask him some questions. He sat next to me, and my tummy gave a little flip-flop as he smiled at me. Strange. Maybe I was getting sick.

"So," he said, "I think you are strangers to Tylwyth Teg?" It was almost impossible to say the name of this town without spitting.

I moved away slightly.

"Yes, that's right," I replied. I wasn't sure how much information to give him, but that much seemed safe enough.

"When your servant finishes cleaning, I'll get her to bring some food from our kitchen to your chamber if you like. My mother is making lunch now," he suggested.

Our servant? We all stared at him and then burst out laughing.

"What's so funny?" he wanted to know.

Persis shook her head, still smiling.

"That's Olive," she explained. "She's not our servant, she's our friend. She just ..." Her voice trailed off uncertainly.

What could she say? That we had followed Bridget to the land of Dralfynia, where we had become characters from fairytales? That our schoolyard enemy had come with us, and suddenly liked cleaning—which was totally out of character?

"She just really likes housework," I butted in. "But some food would be wonderful. And a room with a shower please."

"A shower?" He looked amazed. "Do you mean you want to sleep outside and wait for a brief fall of rain?" It seemed that plumbing in Dralfynia was not going to be what we were used to.

"Um, no thank you. I mean just some hot water to wash in, please," I tried again.

"Okay, we can manage that," said the boy smiling, and my tummy flip-flopped again. "And my mother will have some vegetable stew and bread ready soon."

CHAPTER 23

The boy introduced himself as Aidan. He told us that he was the son of the innkeepers, and that he also worked there.

"I'm the only Aidan in all of Tylwyth Teg, you know," he said. "Most baby boys are called Jack, but my older brother, my father, and my uncle are all called Jack, so it would have been too confusing," he explained.

I thought about the fairy stories and nursery rhymes I knew. Aidan was right—most of the boys were called Jack: Jack be Nimble, Jack and Jill, Little Jack Horner, Jack the Giant Slayer. They didn't have much imagination when it came to naming their sons in Dralfynia.

"Well, I'm called Rory, and I'm the only 'Rory' in my school, too," Rory chimed in. He waved his hands at us. "That's my big sister Sabrina, and that's her friend Persis." A vague look came into Aidan's eyes.

"You look familiar ... as if I should know you," he murmured, "but I don't recognize your names." He shook his head.

We looked at each other. 'Yes, you probably think we should be called Rapunzel, Cinderella, Little Red Riding Hood and Ali Baba,' I thought.

Rory was enjoying some male bonding and chatting away to Aidan.

"Hey Aidan, who were those three men who stared at us as they left?" he asked. Now it was Aidan's turn to laugh.

"Those weren't men," he said, wiping his eyes with the back of his hand. "They were female dwarves. But I admit it's hard to tell the difference."

"So why were they staring at us?" Rory persisted. Aidan responded with a shrug of his shoulders.

"I don't know. We don't get many bloodnuts like you, except in the royal family, of course." Anyone who's watched Rory's famous tantrums or seen him burp his ABCs would know there was nothing royal about him.

"What are 'bloodnuts'?" he asked, suspicious it was an insult.

"It means people with red hair is all," I explained. I turned to Aidan. "Sometimes kids at school tease Rory for the color of his hair and other stuff, and call him mean names." Aidan looked surprised.

"Why?" he asked.

Persis spoke up. "For the same reason they bully me for having dark hair and skin," she said. "Because they are complete—"

"—ly afraid!" I interrupted. "Afraid of anything that's different to them."

We could tell that Aidan had no idea what we were talking about, but, before he could start to quiz us about what bullying was, a ghost walked out of a room at the back of the inn, wiping its hands on an apron.

It wasn't really a ghost; it was a woman who had her hair hidden beneath a white cap and was almost completely covered in flour.

"Jack," she began.

Aidan rolled his eyes.

"Mother, I'm Aidan, remember?" he said gently.

"Sorry dear, force of habit. Now, it's almost lunchtime, so I need you to chop some wood, and then get behind the bar. Those miners will be along any minute." She stopped and stared around the room, which was now gleaming.

Cinderella—sorry, Olive—had fallen asleep on the floor, hugging the edge of the fireplace.

Aidan introduced us, and explained that we were—well, Olive was—working for food and a night's board.

Since The Inn of the Fluffy Kitten was cleaner than it had been for years, Aidan's mother just pursed her lips, nodded once and said, "Fine," and disappeared into what I assumed was the kitchen.

Aidan got to his feet.

"I'd better get on with my work," he said. "Just wait here. I'll bring your lunch out. Mother's been baking," he added, unnecessarily.

We woke Olive up, and waited as patiently as we could for Aidan to reappear. He was only a few minutes and came back with a huge bowl of rich stew filled with vegetables and dumplings, and a basket of golden bread and scones. There wasn't even a hint of sweaty socks. In his pocket he had a couple of carrots.

"For your unicorn," he explained. Clyde poked his head through the tiny glassless window above our heads and accepted the carrots noisily, and then returned to feasting on the weeds that surrounded the inn. We were doing the gardening at the same time as the cleaning.

"He can stay in our stable if you like," Aidan offered. "Although you'll need to muck it out, I'm afraid."

"Sure, that would be great. Thanks," I said. I didn't know what 'mucking out' meant, although it didn't sound like fun. But Clyde was one of us and he needed a safe warm bed for tonight as well.

After the most delicious meal I could remember eating in what seemed like years, we took Clyde to the stable. Our afternoon was spent using pitchforks to pull out soiled straw, hoist it into a wheel barrow, dump it on a compost heap, and then replace it with clean, fresh straw. It sounds like a horrible job, but it felt good to be doing something, and Clyde was happy with his new home.

When we returned to the inn, it was crammed almost to bursting with the strangest people I had ever seen.

CHAPTER 24

We hesitated in the doorway, staring around us in amazement. The three hairy female dwarves were back, sharing a table with something that looked like a talking pile of rocks. It turned out to be a stone troll. Most of one entire wall was occupied by what we guessed was a two-headed giant having an argument with itself. Playing a raucous game of chase were some tiny creatures with wings. Rory thought they might be pixies, elves or fairies.

In another corner, huddled near the fire was a group of blue-skinned, pointy-eared, big-nosed creatures with sharp, snapping teeth. They wore leather kilts and had short swords strapped around their waists. We kept away from them because they smelt bad, real bad, like rotten food. Later, Aidan told us they were goblins, who were not usually welcome in Tylwyth Teg.

"But Mom says their money's as good as anyone else's," he sighed. "So here they are. Mind you," he added, dropping his voice and bending over our table to get closer. He was handing us some food: a huge apple pie and a stone jug full of thick cream.

'Hmm, he has cute freckles on his nose as well as dimples; I hadn't spotted them before,' I thought to myself.

"Mind you," he repeated, "something must be up for there to be so many of them. I heard these ones were on their way to Witchy Wu's place, out in Scary Forest. You might have passed it on your way here?"

We were silent, not daring to meet one another's eye. We didn't technically lie by not telling him that we had been there—and had, in fact, eaten quite a lot of it—but we didn't see the point in advertising that little event.

Aidan took our silence as a no.

"If they're stopping here for the night, then it means the witch has summoned them. I dread to think what wickedness she's plotting now." He handed us a knife to cut the pie and some spoons, and went back to his work. Rory's hand snaked toward the knife and I smacked it away.

"No sharp things, you know the rules," I reminded him.

"Uh, plotting to get revenge on the kids who ate half her house is what I'd guess she's plotting now," Olive mumbled, through a mouthful of thick pastry. She scooped a huge dollop of cream onto her bowl and licked her spoon thoughtfully.

"Well," she said, looking at me. "We're here; we have food and a bed for tonight at least. Now what?" I had been wondering the same thing.

"We need information," I said. "I mean, we know where we've been and where we are. But we need to know where Bridget is, and then we need to know how to get back home."

The truth was, I was starting to feel homesick. I missed my dad. I missed him calling me "the unsinkable SS" as a joke. I missed him making Rory and me grilled cheese and ketchup on white bread—his specialty—for lunch. I missed him making me feel safe.

At the mention of the word "home," Rory's eyes teared up. This had been an adventure for us all. We had been a bit scared. We had been completely out of our depth. We had coped. And now, enough was enough. Bridget was the answer. Problem was, where was she?

"I'll go ask Aidan," I suggested, jumping up.

Behind my back Olive and Persis exchanged a look. Olive mimed a kissy-face and Persis stifled a giggle. I could see them reflected in a highly polished shield, which a surprisingly normal-looking human being wore slung across his back, so I knew what they were doing. I mimed back at them, pointing my index and middle fingers at my eyes and then at their reflections, to show that I was watching them. They burst into laughter at my attempt at being tough. Oh well, I hoped my attempt at being a super-spy would go better.

CHAPTER 25

I wondered how to bring up the subject of my stepmother, the witch. I stood uncertainly at the bar, which was level with my eyebrows. Next to me stood a couple of men. I didn't take any notice of them at first, as I was too busy trying to catch Aidan's eye with the top of my head, but gradually their conversation filtered through. They were talking about the goblins in the corner and were giving them hard stares from time to time.

"They're like thieves in the night," said one man who wore a sack as a tunic. "You never hear them come or go. They shouldn't be allowed in this place." His friend, who had the biggest, bushiest beard I had ever seen nodded his head, dislodging two carrots and a feather from his facial hair.

"Ayup," he agreed.

I mentally translated this to mean: "Yes, you are correct."

"Doing the work of that witch, it's disgusting," continued sack-man. "And those eyes of hers," he added. "One green, one black as sin. They give me the heebie-jeebies."

As I stood there wondering what heebie-jeebies were and how to avoid catching them, a thought dropped into my mind. I knew they weren't talking about Bridget because she had one blue eye, and one brown eye, so they had to be talking about Witchy Wu. Well, well, well—it seemed that witches in Dralfynia all have differently-colored eyes.

The one with the beard noticed me listening in on their conversation, and turned his shaggy face in my direction.

Ulp.

"Ayup?" he enquired.

Okay, here goes. I can be a casual super-spy, I told myself. I fixed an anxious grin on my face.

"Uh, good evening," I squeaked. What had happened to my voice? I hoped Aidan hadn't heard me. I coughed and cleared my throat. I decided to be bold. Something told me that these two guys wouldn't get subtlety.

"So, I couldn't help overhearing your conversation," I said. Well, that's because I was listening as hard as I could. "And I was wondering about another witch with different-colored eyes. Her name is Bridget, Bridget Bishop. Do you ...?" My voice trailed off.

Every single person in the Inn of the Fluffy Kitten had stopped talking and was staring at me. Someone dropped a pottery jug, which smashed loudly to the ground and made me jump. The two men made a point of ignoring me by turning their backs to me and starting to talk about the weather in loud voices.

O.

K.

Something was very wrong. Gradually, people began to talk among themselves again, but the goblins in the corner stared at me for a pretty long time.

One good thing to come out of me somehow sticking my foot in my mouth was that Aidan had noticed me peeping over the bar. He looked at me and jerked his head in the direction of Persis, Olive and Rory. I think he didn't want me to open my mouth again and get us into any more trouble. I shuffled back to our table, flicked my long hair out of the way so I wouldn't trip over it, and scooted in at the end of the bench. Aidan came to join us, carrying a tray of pottery mugs filled with an orange liquid.

"Pumpkin juice," he explained. Then he leaned in and said in a low voice:

"I think we need to talk. Your room is at the top of the stairs, turn left. It's the first door on the left. Drink your juice, then slowly and casually go to your room. Wait for me there. Whatever you do, don't answer the door to anyone but me. Clear?"

We nodded. There was something frightening about his grim face and serious words.

CHAPTER 26

We didn't really want to drink our pumpkin juice. It was bright orange, thick and had shreds of raw pumpkin flesh floating in it. Olive took one look and offered to pay Rory when we got back home if he'd drink hers. He took one sip and offered to pay Persis twice as much to drink his and Olive's. She gulped down all three and then looked at me, with hope in her puppy-dog brown eyes.

I sniffed mine. Nope, not going to happen. I pushed my mug over to her and she beamed as she glugged down the gloopy drink. She set down the mug with a flourish, sighed happily, and let out a small, satisfied belch.

"Yum," she said. I was feeling queasy just watching her, and I hadn't even drunk four cups of pumpkin juice.

"Come on, guys," I said. "We need to get out of here." I pushed my way through the thickening crowd and we hurried up the wooden stairs to a landing of rough wooden planks. It was lined with doors that looked a lot like the doors to Clyde's stable. We turned left and took the first door on the left.

It opened with a blood-curdling groan into a room that sloped steeply down. There were half a dozen small, thin mattresses on the floor. Each one had a gray, fluffy blanket folded neatly at one end but there were no pillows or sheets.

"Oh well," said Persis. "At least it's better than the haystack."

She had a point, and at least Clyde wouldn't try to eat these beds. I sank down on the nearest one, and piled up my hair to make a pillow. It was actually very comfortable.

I pulled my blanket around me and decided that it was the softest, coziest blanket I had ever snuggled into. It was dark gray with little flecks of various other colors. I wondered what animal the wool had come from.

I yawned.

Persis gave another little burp.

Olive had found a pottery basin and jug of water and was trying to wash her hands and face. Rory had piled two mattresses on top of one another and was trying to bounce on them. It felt good to be inside, to be well-fed, warm and private. We had full tummies and we were safe. I began to relax, and my eyelids grew heavy; but as I was about to drift off to sleep, there was a knock at the door. Rory hurried over to open it, but Olive quickly stopped him in his tracks.

"Wait," she hissed at him. Then she spoke louder. "Who is it?" The voice on the other side of the door was muffled but clearly Aidan's.

"It's me, Aidan. Let me in." Rory lifted up the wooden handle, and Aidan slipped in, pushing the door closed behind him.

He frowned when he noticed the two mattresses piled on top of each other, and then again when he saw me already lying down. Embarrassed, I sat up and tried to look as if I had been having a power nap, or thinking about important things with my eyes closed.

Aidan stood with his back to the door and eyed us all.

"I think it's time for you strangers to come clean," he said. No one spoke, but the others all looked at me.

Sheesh, it was up to me again. I wished that someone else would step up once in a while. "Look, this is going to sound very strange," I began.

His face said "I'm listening, and it had better be good."

So I told him the story.

As I went through the facts, my face burned. He would definitely think I was crazy.

When I explained that Bridget Bishop was my and Rory's stepmother, and that we had been caught up in a spell from a different world, his eyes widened so much that I worried they might pop out from his skull.

Then I made it worse by explaining how we had accidentally got stuck in Scary Forest, eaten Witchy Wu's house, and followed prompts from a talking tree and Clyde's horn to get us to the town of Tylwyth Teg.

Aidan took a few minutes to absorb our tale. Who wouldn't? Even though we had lived it, I don't think any of us really believed it. I think we all thought we were going to wake up the next day with the words 'Boy, I had the weirdest dream,' on our lips.

"I expect you want to return to your own kingdom?" he asked, frowning. I could hardly believe he was taking us seriously. Thoughts of TV, hot showers, potato chips, Internet, windows with glass in, cars and public transport, our families, jeans and sneakers, and proper mattress with proper bedding filled our minds. Heck yes, we wanted to return to our own kingdom.

"Yes, that's the plan," I said, still imagining myself with a huge soda, a bucket of popcorn, and the TV remote in my hand.

"You're right; Bridget is the answer. As a witch, she understands the spell she used that brought you here. Because you all arrived here together, you will have to return together. That's the only way such a magic spell will work. But you must be careful. In this land, she is a criminal wanted by the prince and his men."

CHAPTER 27

"I knew it!" I told myself. I had known all along that there was something untrustworthy about that woman. She was a witch and now I learned she was a criminal as well. My Uncle Don had been right when he warned me against her. I curled my hands into fists at the thought of her worming her way into my poor dad's heart, and almost into mine and Rory's.

Aidan pulled a tattered piece of rough brown paper from a pocket in his tunic and unfolded it. It was a 'wanted' poster for Bridget Bishop. She was accused of treason against the Prince, and the price on her head was one hundred pumpkins.

"There are people—bad people—loyal to the prince, who would use your links with Bridget to try to capture her," continued Aidan.

'So what?' I thought, then I remembered that the four of us and Clyde needed her help to get back home.

"To find her, you will need to hide from those loyal to the Beast with Nine Fingers," he said

Huh? We all straightened up and looked at Aidan. That definitely sounded creepy. "The what with nine whats?" I said.

"It's what they call the Prince," he explained. Then he sighed. "You really don't know anything about Dralfynia do you?" he asked.

We shook our heads. Persis shook her head a bit too much and burped again. That pumpkin juice was playing havoc with her tummy.

Aidan came across the room and sat next to Rory on the double-decker mattress.

"I'll try to make a long history as short as I can," he told us. We settled down to listen. I always liked story-time when I was in kindergarten, and now I felt as though I was four years old and my dad was reading me fairy tales—but this time, they were real.

Aidan began his story.

"Dralfynia has always been a small, peaceful kingdom. Our main crop is pumpkins, but we also mine for precious metals and gemstones. Our capital city is Timaru, and the Royal Castle stands on a hill overlooking the city. Our ruling family is the di Kristi family, and, until now, they have reigned with kindness for generations.

It is our tradition that the king and queen retire when they wish and pass the throne to their eldest child. King Michael and Queen Hazel had two children. Princess Heidi's three years older than her brother—he's the one we call the Beast. She, Princess Heidi was always popular with us. The people loved her, but no one has seen her for the past twelve years. Her disappearance broke her parents' hearts, and the spirit of many a proud Dralfynian. After years of searching, the king and queen felt defeated. They chose retirement and passed power to the queen's sister, Duchess Yvonne, until the princess could be found. There have been many rumors about what happened to Princess Heidi. Some say that she joined a traveling circus, others that she married a commoner and is too ashamed to face her parents. Most believe that she is already dead. Everyone has been looking for the princess since I was a child.

Nowadays, the king and queen live near here in a wood cabin on the Island of Merthyr."

Aidan paused in his tale to point out of the window, across the dark village. In the twilight we could see the glimmers of waves that reflected the moon as it began to rise.

"That's Lake Pleasant; the Isle of Merthyr is fifteen minutes hard rowing from the shore. They take in stray cats, give them a loving home, and spin yarn from their fur. In fact, these blankets have come from them." He sighed and returned to his seat next to Rory, fingering the blanket absent-mindedly as he spoke.

"These events have split our land. We are waiting to hear who will rule if the princess cannot be found. If his parents agree to it, the Beast will become king. Dralfynians such as the goblins, the rich land owners and Witchy Wu would be glad but most of us would suffer under his cruelty."

Again, he paused and looked at us, weighing up whether to trust us or not.

"There are some of us, people like Duchess Yvonne, your step mother and many of the peasants who are still loyal to the princess. Perhaps she will return. Perhaps she has children who would be the heirs to the throne. We do what we can to protect Dralfynia from the Beast and his followers, but it must be done in secret for fear of the suffering that the prince would inflict on our families."

CHAPTER 28

Wow, that was a lot of information. Aidan fell silent, waiting for our response. We hardly knew where to start with our questions, but trust Rory to ask the one we all wanted to know the most.

"Why is he called 'the Beast with Nine Fingers'?"

If Aidan was expecting us to ask about the mysterious royal family or the politics of Dralfynia, he was too polite to show his disappointment.

"Because he is not a very nice man, and because he lost one of his fingers," he explained shortly.

"Yes, but how did he lose his finger? And which one was it?" Rory can be quite bloodthirsty. Aidan gave a little sigh of resignation.

"In a fight with his sister," he explained.

Really? Go the princess—striking a blow for big sisters everywhere, I thought.

Rory wasn't happy to hear this, though, and frowned at Aidan.

"So did she cheat then, when they were playing rough? Like by too much tickling?" he demanded, shooting a look at me. I looked innocently up at the ceiling. Aidan shook his head.

"There are three special magic objects in Dralfynia; they can only be controlled by those of royal blood and whoever wishes to be the ruler must have them. One is a flying carpet, one is a pair of glass slippers and the last is a magic slingshot. They have disappeared in the recent troubles, but many years ago, when the prince was trying to snatch the glass slipper from his sister, the heel snapped off and sliced through his finger." He paused, made slow eye-contact with each of us and held up his left hand with the index finger bent down. "It was this finger," he said, in a deep voice. For a second we all believed he was the evil prince we had been hearing so much about, until he popped his finger back up and smiled broadly at us.

"Hmm, sounds like cheating to me, attacking her little brother with a dangerous shoe," Rory muttered.

"Rory, it was just an accident," I said, then I faced Aidan. I had a question, too. "About Bridget. You said she was a criminal, and a witch?"

He nodded. "So how can she be on the side of the princess? Is the princess really the 'bad guy' in all this?"

Aidan gasped, horrified at what I had suggested. He shook his head.

"No," he said. "The princess wanted to be like the rest of us," he said. "She didn't want to obey all the court rules, but she was always incredibly kind to the people and animals of Dralfynia. The prince? All he cares about is power and money." Aidan's eyes blazed with hatred. Whatever this prince had done, he had made a staunch enemy of the innkeeper's young son.

"As for Bridget," he continued. "Yes, she's a witch. But a good witch. A white witch. As you are related to one, you will know that witches are born, not made. Magic runs in families, although you can tell a witch by their different-colored eyes."

Yep, I had worked that part out already at least.

"Bridget was an old friend of the princess," Aidan explained. "And Duchess Yvonne is Heidi's godmother, so now Bridget and the Duchess are allies."

"Godmother?" asked Olive. "Like, fairy godmother?" Aidan wrinkled his forehead.

"No," he said. "She's just a regular person who was made Heidi's godmother when she was born."

"So if the king and queen agree and the Beast can find those three things then it's a done deal?"

Aidan shrugged. "If he finds the three objects and he can control them, he can appoint himself ruler, although he would be wise to have his parents' approval. The people of Dralfynia love and respect them above all others. The Beast has sent search parties across the land to look for the flying carpet, and unless the princess or her heirs return, then the kingdom will be at the mercy of a king who cares nothing for his subjects and will tax us to starvation."

Aidan looked at Rory and me.

"There have been other tales too," he said slowly. "It has been said that Duchess Yvonne sent Bridget away to other lands to look for the princess. Your step-mother been seen disappearing and then returning regularly for the past two years. If she's back in Dralfynia, I suspect she will be at the Royal Castle in Timaru, reporting to Duchess Yvonne."

I thought about what he had said. If you take away all that prince and throne stuff, we finally we knew where we would find Bridget Bishop Summers, so that we could make her take us back to Melas, and that was what really mattered.

CHAPTER 29

Persis raised her hand as if she was at school. She'd been very quiet while Aidan was talking, but I had noticed her fidgeting a lot.

"Hey, all that pumpkin juice has ... uh, you know," she apologized. She opened the door with some reluctance. We all knew why. The toilets were in a shed outside, near the stable block. They were basic to say the least, nothing more than a long plank of wood with holes cut in it, which had been placed on top of a box. The box sat over a deep ditch full of—well, you can guess what. We had all been there earlier in the day. It had been smelly and gross, but it was worse for me because of the long dress and all the hair. Persis had to help me hold things out of the way when I went, which was deeply embarrassing for us both.

Nevertheless, four mugs of pumpkin juice couldn't be denied, so she hurried past Aidan out into the landing, and we heard her running as fast as possible down the stairs.

"Tomorrow I'll get you a map of Dralfynia and show you the route to take to Timaru and the Royal Castle. If you hire a boat, you can row across Lake Pleasant instead of walking around it, so it should only take you three days to get to the castle. I'll give you a letter from Ma and Da to show to other innkeepers when you need somewhere to stay on your journey."

Olive was obviously feeling a bit better. As Aidan made to leave, she laid a hand on his arm and looked deeply into his eyes.

"Thanks, Aidan. I really appreciate all your help. I'm sure the others do too," she smiled up at him.

As Olive, she had been working on her flirting for the school year. Unfortunately, as Cinderella, she didn't have access to a tooth brush, paste, floss or mouthwash and Aidan took a step back.

"Oh, you're welcome," he said, flustered, before backing out of the room as fast as he politely could.

"Sleep well, see you in the morning," he flung back over his shoulder as he turned away. "Oh, and remember. Be careful—and trust no one."

I lay down again; my head was spinning. Was Bridget one of the good guys or not? Why was she looking for a princess in our little town? Could we even trust Aidan? To be brutally honest, did any of us really care about what went on in this, to put it politely, rather unsophisticated kingdom? And who would have thought that cat fluff would make such wonderfully soft, deliciously cozy blankets?

Across the room I heard Rory and Olive both snuggling in. We talked for a couple of minutes, but the stress, excitement and hard work had caught up with all of us. Tomorrow would be soon enough to make plans. I was starting to drift off to sleep when the door handle rattled. Someone knocked at the door.

"Whassup?" I asked sleepily.

"Brina? It's me, Persis. Please open the door." Groggily I got to my feet and pulled the door wide open.

Framed in the doorway stood my best friend. She looked terrified. A vicious-looking blade was held to her bare throat. Behind her stood three goblins.

CHAPTER 30

Silently, they shoved Persis into the room and followed her, latching the door behind them. Persis started to cry.

"I'm so sorry; they got me when I was coming out of the toilet. I was so scared they were going to hurt me; I did what they told me to. And they ... they threatened to hurt Clyde." She burst into tears.

I pulled her into my arms and held her tight.

"It's okay, it's okay," I soothed. "We'd all have done the same thing in your situation," I said. "Right guys?"

Rory said yes.

Olive didn't reply.

I narrowed my eyes at her. She narrowed hers back at me. Then she decided this was not the time for an eye-narrowing contest and boldly walked over to the biggest of the goblins. "You're being ridiculous. Don't you know who I am? My father is Jonathon Ayres; he's a very rich man."

In this stressful situation, she had reverted back to her usual Ayres and Graces self, except for the fact that she was wearing rags and was filthy. The goblin laughed—by which I mean that he made a noise like water going down a partly blocked drain.

Then he slapped her face.

We all gasped in shock. None of the adults in our lives would ever hit a child, and we couldn't believe what we had seen. Poor Olive held her face, and her eyes teared in pain. The delicate freckles that were sprinkled across her nose (and which she usually tried to hide) darkened as she flushed in shock. But to her credit, she did not back down. She came over to join Persis and me, her back straight and her walk steady. Rory slunk across to join us. I glanced over to the far corner where Persis had flung her axe. Even if we could get to it, it would be one axe against three sharp swords, which wasn't a fair contest. I decided to try and talk our way out of the situation.

"What is it? What do you want?" I asked. "We're just travelers. We don't mean anyone any harm. And we have no money." My voice trembled as I spoke.

"No 'arm? You're 'ouse-eating vaaandals and my king knows someone what would pay a great deal to get 'er 'ands on you four," drawled the biggest goblin. After a few seconds of trying to work out his accent, we realized he meant that Witchy Wu would pay the Goblin King to have us handed over to her because we had vandalized her house by eating it. We were in serious trouble.

The three goblins had all pulled out short, sharp, and very pointy swords. They stood between us and the door. We were trapped.

As we had been snuggling down in our beds, we had been aware of the night getting darker and the people in the inn settling down, as all around it grew quieter and quieter. Now it was completely dark, and nobody was around to help us.

The biggest and ugliest of the blue-faced goblins suddenly gestured toward the door with his knife.

"Now," he hissed. "Move now. Make a sound and I'll slit your throats. Cause trouble, and your unicorn gets it. Ee's locked into 'is stable and won't be coming to rescue you."

After we had wiped the goblin-spit from our faces, we moved immediately, as instructed. These guys meant business. One of them opened our door and peered left and right along the dim landing. There was no one around. He led the way down the stairs, across the deserted main room of the inn, and out into the silent night. The other two goblins were behind us, swords at the ready. Their attention never wavered for a second. Say what you like about goblins, but you can't doubt their focus and professionalism—unfortunately. Outside a black shadow started to move, and a fourth goblin materialized from the darkness. He was leading a pair of huge oxen, who were pulling an open cart behind them. It was our transport for the night. But to where?

CHAPTER 31

Before we could so much as squeak like the frightened mice we felt like, rough sacks had been thrown over our heads and the tops of our bodies. A rope was tied around each of our waists to hold the sacks in place, and we were picked up and lifted into the cart. At least the canvas was a barrier against the foul smell of the goblins.

We were allowed to sit up, but it was difficult to keep our balance as the cart lurched forward, and I felt someone fall against me. I pushed back so that whoever it was could sit up again.

"Thanks," said a muffled voice, which I thought belonged to Persis.

"You're welcome," I replied. Goodness knows why we were being so polite when we were so terrified—but we were.

"Silence!" a goblin ordered.

We shut up. For a while, at least.

It was just awful. The sacks had been used to carry muddy pumpkins and stank of dirt.

Little chunks of dry mud flaked off from the inside of the sacks and landed on our faces and in our ears, hair, and mouths. I tried to keep my mouth and eyes shut. I breathed through my nose as much as I could.

The cart was made of rough wood and every time we hit a rut in the road, we were bumped up and down violently; this caused our spines to bang against the sides of the cart, and made our legs and backsides slam into the floor of the cart. My muscles ached from the effort of keeping upright, and all the jolting was making me feel sick. I wondered how poor Olive was coping.

Then I heard Rory snuffling on the other side of me. He's so deliberately aggravating for almost every single one of his waking minutes that I often forget that he's just a kid. If I was scared, he must have been terrified.

"Um, excuse me," I piped up, my voice quavering.

"Silence!" was the reply.

At least the sack was protecting me from goblin-spit.

"Look, if we promise to be quiet, can you take the sacks off?"

"Silence!"

"Please, we can hardly breathe." I tried begging.

"Silence!"

Oh please, this was getting boring. Didn't they know any other words?

Then Olive joined in with the wheedling and complaining. Well, she is excellent at it, after all.

"Please? Please take the sacks off? I feel totally sick, and someone keeps bashing into me. Plus the sacks stink really bad."

"That's right," chimed in Persis. "We can hardly breathe, and if we do, bits of mud go up our noses. There's really no need for it. We promise to be quiet when you do take them off. And if our arms are tied up, then we won't be able to escape."

Oh great. Giving them ideas to stop us escaping wasn't her best move, but good old Rory sealed the deal.

"Wahhhh!" he began. I knew the start of a good old-fashioned tantrum when I heard it. The volume increased. "WAHHH!" he roared. "LETMEOUT—LETMEOUT—LETMEOUT!" It went on for some few minutes before, finally, I heard a sword being pulled from its sheath; my sack was jerked backward, and I saw a blade slice through the rough material—just a few millimeters from my face.

I didn't care that I had almost lost my nose. I gulped in clean, fresh air and shook myself like a dog so that the shredded sack fell from my head and shoulders. We were still bound around the waist, but just being able to see one another and taste the night air felt like freedom.

CHAPTER 32

I did a quick check. Olive looked distinctly green, even by the dim light cast by a swaying lantern held by one of the goblins. Persis had fared a little better. Her hood had protected her from the worst of the mud and given her a little breathing room, too. Rory's face was scarlet and wet from tears. He looked furious and petrified at the same time. I had no idea what I looked like, but I assumed my thick hair was matted with dry dirt.

I looked around us. The cart was open, so I could see the surrounding countryside. We had been traveling for what seemed like half an hour, and I was expecting to see the fields near Scary Forest again, or even the start of the forest itself. Instead, I saw an expanse of flat, black water, so still that it reflected the night sky perfectly.

I figured that it was the Lake Pleasant Aidan had told us about. We must have been following its shoreline as we travelled away from the village. I brightened up. Aidan had mentioned that we needed to cross it if we wanted to get to Timaru to find Bridget. Perhaps being kidnapped by goblins was going to work out okay after all. Yes, perhaps. And perhaps I would become Miss Popular at school and Rory would win Best Student.

The ox cart lurched to a sudden stop, tilting us all over onto our sides. The driver and the other three goblins leapt nimbly into the back of the cart. They each grabbed one of us and flung us over their backs as if we were nothing more than the sacks we still had dangling from our waists.

"Ooof." The air was knocked from me as my chest and lungs were bashed against my goblin's bony shoulder. His sharp claws cut into my legs as he held me in place, and my face kept banging into the goblin's lumpy blue back as he jumped to the ground and then ran lightly toward a jetty. It was a horrible experience, but the worst thing was having my nose so near to his armpit. I decided that they hadn't invented goblin deodorant yet.

I tried to bend my neck up to see what was happening, but it was too dark and my goblin seemed to be bounding along at high speed. In a few seconds, he had sprinted along the jetty, lifted me into the air, and was holding me at arm's length, by my ankles, over the cold, dark water. As I dangled there, the muscles in my legs and back ached from the strain of trying to keep myself straight, and the dank, chill of the water rose up like a fog that stroked my face. I began to wriggle and thrash around like a poor, tortured fish on a hook. The goblin leaned further over, still holding me by my ankles. Then he let go.

I tried to scream but I didn't have time. The lake had looked deep, and with our arms tied, there was no way we could swim. The goblins were going to drown us all in revenge for eating a few sweets and some chunks of gingerbread. I would never see my dad again, and he would never know what had happened to his children. Bridget would return to Melas and he would never know that he had married a witch. I would never go to the prom; I would never go to college and have a career. The pony that filled my dreams would never be mine. My eyes burned with tears as I plummeted down, head first.

CHAPTER 33

Whack! Instead of splashing into the water, I smashed hard into the bottom of a wooden boat. It was only slightly better than landing in the water would have been, and my eyes smarted with more tears from the shock and the stabbing pain where I had landed on my shoulder and hip. How could this get worse? We were in a strange land, we had been captured by goblins who were in the pay of an evil witch, and I had been thrown so hard into a wooden boat that I was bruised and aching.

I soon found out how it could get worse: the goblins threw Olive in on top of me.

"Ooof," she said.

"Get. Off. Me." I said. For a girl who obsessively watched her diet, she was a surprisingly healthy weight. I wriggled around and shoved her away with my good shoulder. Luckily, I had the sense to haul myself out of the drop zone by imitating a worm. Olive didn't.

"Ooof," she gasped again as Rory was thrown right on top of her, forcing all the air from her lungs. She lay on her back as he struggled to get off of her, her breath coming in short, desperate pants as she struggled to fill her lungs again.

Before I could shout a warning, Persis tumbled down on top of them both. As they all lay there like stunned jellyfish, flapping their bound legs and calling one another names, I realized why I was the leader of our sorry little troop. Well, until the goblins had taken over, that is.

With frightening efficiency (I was guessing they had captured and held prisoner lots of people before us), the goblins hauled the other three up to sitting positions on the planks of rough wood that ran like benches across one end of the boat. As the biggest goblin jumped down, the boat lurched and tipped to one side, and we all slid toward the water. We screamed and tried to right ourselves by using our back and leg muscles.

"You have to untie us," I pleaded. "We'll fall in and drown if you don't."

Two of the goblins shrugged. They could not care less if we drowned. A third goblin sniggered. He sounded like he would enjoy seeing that show. The leader had a little more intelligence than the others; he looked me up and down while he thought about it.

"I don't think Witchy Wu would be pleased with you if you captured us and then lost us overboard, would she?" I hoped like crazy that he understood the ideas of logic, and consequences.

He did. He raised his sword and sliced it downward, directing it right at me. I gasped in terror, but his aim was perfect: with a few deft slices, he severed the ropes around our bodies and arms, and blood rushed to our fingertips again.

The painful sensation of pins and needles in our arms was all we could focus on for the next few minutes, as we waggled our hands and rubbed our arms. We didn't even notice that the boat had slid from its moorings until it began to shoot across the still water of Lake Pleasant, rowed by the two powerful goblins who were seated behind us.

We had coped with enough goblin-spit on our face for one day, so none of us spoke to our captors. Instead we stared around us as we sped, hour after hour, across the lake. The moon had long since slipped away over the horizon and had been replaced by the ever- lightening gray of early dawn. We could no longer make out the dim shape of Tylwyth Teg, home of the only friend we had found since we had arrived in Dralfynia. I wondered what Aidan would think when he found our room empty. I supposed that he would think we had gone on our way early; that had been our plan after all. I hoped he would be a little hurt that I hadn't said goodbye.

Eventually I began to notice little glimmers of light coming from the windows of the houses that were scattered along the lake shore. For the people of Dralfynia, a new day was beginning. I wondered what they would do. They might go to work in the fields or bake bread or go to school: all normal, safe, happy activities. But none of them would be starting their day as the captive of goblins.

I felt afraid and very sorry for myself.

CHAPTER 34

A dark mass appeared to the side of us as the flat land began to give way to hillier ground. The head goblin started hissing orders at the two rowers. He seemed to be urging them to go faster and faster. I guessed that he wanted to get us past the farms before anyone who might want to help us could see us in the dawn's light. I looked at the distance between the boat and the shore and thought about jumping in and swimming for help. Persis could do it, I was certain. I didn't know if I would manage or not, but I suspected that neither Olive nor Rory would make it if we tried to escape that way. Then I thought about screaming for help, but we were so far away that it was unlikely that anyone would hear us— and anyway, the goblins were happy to lash out at the slightest sign of defiance. I sighed and slumped down in my bench seat. I couldn't think of anything that we could do except wait and see what happened next.

Beside me Rory shivered. It was cold that early in the morning, especially out on the water. I put my arm around him and held him closer to me. He snuggled in. Dad would have been so proud to see us being nice to one another. Believe me, it was a rare occurrence.

Dad. Would I ever see him again? How would he cope without me? Who would tell him when he had his jerseys on inside out, or when he had froth from a hot chocolate on his upper lip? Who would be in the background, making sure I was okay, even though I was twelve and could look after myself really?

I sniffed and a single tear rolled down my cheek and plopped onto Rory's head. The tear soaked through his fine red hair and onto his scalp.

He raised his head and looked at me.

"Cry-baby," he said, but I knew he didn't mean it.

The journey only lasted another couple of hours but it seemed so much longer. The boat was cramped and uncomfortable, and we were hungry and thirsty, but too scared to move or complain.

As we skimmed over the water, I watched the scenery change on the distant shorelines. The low hills and lush pasture gave way to densely-forested mountains. One peak soared above the rest, so high that it was tipped with snow and, as the boat changed direction, I realized that we were heading straight for it. Whatever was on that mountain, it wasn't the gingerbread cottage we had eaten—so maybe, just maybe, it would turn out okay.

CHAPTER 35

Or maybe not. The goblin rowers brought us into a narrow inlet that sloped up to a stony shore. They leapt out onto dry land, leaned down, and hauled us out by our arms—which, by the way, really hurts your armpits. Soon, the four of us and our four captors were crowded onto a narrow beach, looking up at a trail that was barely wide enough to walk along. The head goblin turned and followed the ledge, leading the way for the rest of us to follow.

For such ungainly-looking creatures, goblins are very nimble. We four humans stumbled along, afraid of tripping and falling as the path narrowed until it was no more to a winding ledge that zigzagged up the mountain. One goblin kept turning and hissing at us to try and make us hurry, but we were too clumsy in our movements. By now the morning was light and we could see the ground more clearly. That made it easier to step over rocks and avoid holes in the ground.

Unfortunately, we could also see the fang-like rocks that lay at the bottom of the sharp drop below us, waiting for one of us to take just one false step. Although we hugged the side of the mountain as we walked, there were several occasions when each of us almost lost our footing.

Soon, our legs began to tire, especially Rory's. It was a steep climb. After sitting cramped in the cart and then the boat for so long, we were stiff.

"We need a rest. And some food. Please let us just sit down for a few minutes," I begged. The head goblin didn't even turn back to look at me, but I saw the back of his head shake from side to side vehemently, and caught the words he flung back at me.

"Soon, soon." Soon what? Soon food and rest? Soon something worse?

It turned out to be both, but the "worse" came first. Of course.

After two hours of climbing we were so exhausted that we could hardly put one foot in front of the other. Olive's feet were bleeding where her leaves had worn away, and I could feel my knees trembling as if they would give way once and for all.

We rounded a final bend and came to an open space scattered with boulders and tufts of coarse grass, and even some tiny alpine flowers. The view was amazing. Far below us, on my right, I could see the blue water of Lake Pleasant shimmer and sparkle in the bright sunshine. If I really craned my neck backward, I could see what must be the Island of Merthyr as a dark smudge, and I could even make out the town of Tylwyth Teg. Peering around the curve of the mountainside in front of me, and to my left, I saw distant forests—but also farms and a large collection of buildings that could only be the capital city, Timaru. Behind it, rose another mountain, which I guessed was where the Royal Castle was. And inside it? Bridget. We were getting nearer!

But, directly ahead, just a few feet away, gaped the wide mouth of a cave. Two more goblins stood outside—they were obviously sentries. Each one held a spear upright and stood very still, although their eyes took everything in.

The goblin in charge of us hurried over to them, his feet flapping on the rocks. He had an energetic discussion with one of them: he danced around, waved his arms, pointed at us, shouted, and—of course—spat a lot. The sentry goblin flicked his head slightly, indicating that we could all enter the cave.

Too tired to wonder what we had gotten ourselves into, we plodded along, following the goblin to wherever he was leading us now.

The cave was surprisingly spacious and some light filtered through from chimney-like openings above us. Small tunnels ran off it at ragged intervals, and the ceiling soared high above us. All around were piles of junk: old trunks, broken crockery, weapons, clothing, rugs, and discarded food. It was just as well that the cave was so large—the smell was terrible, even with fresh air coming in.

Goblins slept in piles on top of one another, heaped up like puppies, or they sat chewing chunks of meat and drinking from leather cups. Two smaller goblins ran past. They seemed to be youngsters and, like ordinary children, they were playing chase, hurdling over furniture, and throwing a ball back and forth between them. Rory took a step toward them; it looked like fun. They laughed and gurgled, and dodged the reaching hands of grown-up goblins. Then one of them dropped the ball, which ended the game. The ball rolled near to us: it wasn't a ball at all. It was a skull. The larger of the young goblins caught hold of his playmate, angry that his fun had stopped. He bared needle-sharp teeth and sank them hard into his friend's leg. Black blood spurted out, and the smaller goblin wept and wailed, but no one came to help.

It was noisy, smelly and chaotic. My heart sank. These creatures were awful. Ahead of us, we could see two large chairs on a raised platform which stood at the far end of the cave. On one of the chairs sat a huge, and extremely fat, goblin, who had a tiny crown—similar to my own— balanced on his head. He grinned at us, and showed a mouth filled with blackened, decaying teeth.

Next to him sat a woman with jet-black hair piled on top of her head and held in place with ornate combs and chopsticks. She wore a black silk robe with wide sleeves, held in place with a broad band of crimson cloth. On one of her shoulders was a bat, sitting as proud as a pirate's parrot. She had one black eye and one green eye.

CHAPTER 36

Well, well, well, this must be our old friend, the wicked Witchy Wu, owner of the infamous gingerbread cottage. She and the Goblin King were buddies, and it was his minions that had been sent to trap us and bring us back to her. Didn't I tell you it got worse before it got better?

We just stood there. We had no idea what to do or say, so we did and said nothing. Witchy Wu stood up. Her face was painted white, and her crimson lips matched her belt. Stark black eyebrows and eyes rimmed with heavy black make-up completed her look. She was terrifying.

She walked slowly over to us; her mouth was twisted into a smile so evil that it turned my blood cold. When she grinned, we could see her teeth. They were green stumps, rotten from all the sugary food her cottage was made from. She went first to Rory and stroked a long, pointed fingernail down his cheek, leaving a red mark where it had dragged across his skin. Then she walked around the four of us, looking each of us up and down. The hairs on my skin prickled as she approached me. I could smell her foul breath and see the loathing in her eyes. I looked away. Her bat stood up, flapped its wings, and hissed at me.

She turned her back on us and faced the Goblin King.

"Azul, these children are too skinny," she proclaimed. Her voice grated like fingers being dragged down an old-fashioned blackboard. "They need fattening up." King Azul waved his hand at the goblins that had brought us here and we were gripped by our arms and dragged away along a side passageway that lead off from the main cavern.

Witchy Wu's words had filled us with icy panic. We struggled and kicked as best we could, but we were exhausted and they were too strong. The passageway floor was littered with boulders and rocks, and our feet kept being dragged over them, stubbing and bruising our toes and bending the tips of Rory's slippers.

Then it got better.

They threw us into our own little cave, which was still little more than a junk pile, and one goblin stood guard at the opening while the others disappeared for a few minutes.

When they came back, they carried a dirty, leather tray piled high with cheese, fried potatoes, and cakes oozing with cream. Not a vegetable or a piece of fruit in sight. It was great.

We ate with our hands, cramming food into our mouths like wild beasts. Even Olive, the most refined of us all, actually growled once when I took a donut she had her eye on.

Finally, we sat back; we were stuffed. Olive obviously felt refreshed because she began to prowl around our cave while the rest of us watched her. As she went, she started sorting out the junk and tidying things away. She was really rocking this Cinderella thing. I settled down on a wooden chest to rest but she soon tipped up the chest, and me with it, onto the floor. Huffing and puffing, she dragged it to the side of the cave, where she had collected the rest of the chests and barrels. She had placed a large barrel in the center and smaller chests around it to make a dining area. Glancing inside one smaller barrel, she found gold platters, goblets, knives and forks. She took them out and laid them on her 'table.' Persis came up behind her and stared inside the barrel: it was full of gold coins and chains.

Excitedly, Persis began to explore the cave, peeking into sacks and kicking away rolled- up rugs.

"This is a treasure store," she called out, lifting up a gold shield and fixing it experimentally to her arm. It weighed too much for her to even raise her arm, so she dumped it again.

"Whoa, look at the size of this diamond," she said, holding up a sparkling gem the size of a golf ball. Olive took it from her and placed it on a shelf that ran at head height around the rim of the entire cave. Anything pretty that caught her eye went on that shelf. It already held a lamp, just like the one Aladdin might have used to summon his genie along with several precious gemstones, a few silver candelabras and even an ornamental shoe carved from clear crystal. It didn't matter to her if an object was damaged: if she liked the look of it, she placed it lovingly onto her shelf.

Then she turned her attention to the richly-woven rugs. She unrolled them, flicked them to get the dust off, and laid them on the floor. Now that was more like it: somewhere we could lie down in some comfort at last.

CHAPTER 37

"Ouch," said Olive, licking her hand. She kicked at the last rug in the pile. "This dumb carpet bit me," she complained. I had been feeling guilty at just sitting around and watching her. As a princess Rapunzel would not have had to do housework, I reasoned. Sighing, I got up and went to the rug. It was the smallest of them all, and not at all deep and luxurious like some of the others. It was dull blue and red with intricate patterns woven into it.

I bent down, picked it up, and gave it a vigorous shake, in case there were any bugs in it. Then I laid it on the ground with a dramatic gesture.

"There you are," I said kindly, feeling proud that I had contributed. Olive stood on the rug, but nothing happened. She bent to pick it up and move it closer to the other rugs, and squeaked once more.

"It bit me again," she protested. I looked at her hand. It did have a red mark where she had tried to pick up the rug. Weird.

But to be honest, I didn't care. None of us did. The goblin that had brought us the food had reappeared and dumped a pitcher of some sweet-tasting liquid on the floor. We had to share it, but we were so thirsty that each of us could hardly wait for a turn. Rory tried to grab the pitcher while Persis was still drinking, and jolted her elbow, which caused some of the precious liquid to be spilled on the floor. It almost started a fight between them. After we had drunk our fill, we sank down onto the pile of carpets and curled up, just like the piles of goblins we had seen. My hair had grown a couple of inches each day we had been there, so I spread it out for everyone to use as a pillow. We began to drift off to sleep.

"If only I had a broom," Olive murmured.

Persis yawned her reply. "Ask Witchy Wu; I bet she flew here on one."

"She wasn't what I expected from a witch," I commented. I had imagined her to be green-skinned, warty, and wearing a pointed black hat.

"She's a Chinese witch," Olive explained. "I've seen pictures of them in books. Oh yeah, and 'wu' is the Chinese name for a witch," she added, realizing now how rude her "wu who?" pun had been, but she was fast asleep before she could finish her thought.

I don't know how long we slept for, but it must have been hours. I was the last to wake up. I forced my eyes to open because I could hear the others moving around and talking quietly.

"You should have been Sleeping Beauty, not Rapunzel," Olive remarked, when she saw that I was awake.

"Yeah? Well you should have been ..." It's so annoying when you can't think of a good reply to a put-down, isn't it? She ignored me. I am kind of grumpy when I first wake up, to be fair. I sat up and flicked my hair back off my face, which took quite some time.

"Look at your hair," Persis exclaimed. I looked. It had grown even more. Now it was way, way past my feet. I searched the cave for some rope or string; in the end, I found a long piece of twine, which I used to create a long, heavy braid, so that I could at least walk around, but it gave me a headache anyway.

I went across to the little dining area Olive had created and sat down with everyone else. On the middle barrel was another huge platter of high-sugar, high-fat, high-carbohydrate food. I picked up a chocolate éclair and slurped the cream that oozed out of the end. I scarfed it down in three huge bites and licked the melted chocolate off my fingers. I realized that the other three were looking at me.

"What?"

"You do know that's what the witch wants, don't you? She wants us to eat and eat, and not be able to escape." Olive pointed out. "All this food was here when we woke up and we decided not to eat it."

"Yeah, of course. But we don't know when we'll have our next meal, so it makes sense to me if we stock up while we can," I said, reaching for another éclair. That was all Rory and Persis needed, and they started to tuck in, too. Olive watched for a couple more minutes, with an expression of agonized uncertainty on her face. Then she too snatched up some fluffy white bread, thick with butter and crammed it into her mouth.

"So, what were you guys talking about?" I asked, spraying a few crumbs their way.

"Escaping," said Persis between mouthfuls.

I took a sip of the sweet yellow liquid.

"Cool, what's the plan?" I asked, and yawned. I couldn't be tired already, surely? I checked out the entrance to our cave. There wasn't a goblin in sight.

Olive took the pitcher of drink from me and had a glug herself before passing it to Persis who drank deeply before answering me.

"Well, we think that the goblins are pretty slack at guarding us. If we wait until dark, we can sneak out. And I spotted an opening at the far end of the passage that this cave is in. If we get to that, we can climb down and be as far away as possible before they even know we're awaaaaaaaaake," she said, yawning hugely before she could finish speaking.

Olive slapped the drink from Persis' hand, spilling most of it to the floor. We stared at her in horror. That was the only thing we had to drink. What was she up to?

CHAPTER 38

"It's a sleeping drink of some kind," she explained. "I watched you two. Just a few seconds after you drank it, you started to yawn. It explains why we all slept so heavily, even though we should have been too afraid to sleep, considering that we're captives in the lair of the Goblin King." Her face was flushed and her eyes were bright with excitement.

"So I guess that explains why we aren't guarded, doesn't it?" I suggested.

Olive leaned forward.

"This works right into our plan. If they think we have actually drunk this stuff, they'll assume we are fast asleep, and they'll leave us alone. We just have to take it in turns to keep awake and keep watch. When the person on guard thinks the coast is clear, they will wake the rest of us up, and we can escape."

I couldn't think of a flaw, and I couldn't think of a better idea, so I was forced to agree it with her.

"I'll take the first watch if you like," Rory piped up. "I haven't had anything to drink." Since we three girls were all yawning our heads off already, it seemed sensible to let him do that. Soon, we were snuggled up on our rugs again, and I fell into a deep, deep sleep right away.

I woke up to find Rory pinching my nose.

"Stop it," I said, annoyed.

"Shush, you were snoring," he whispered. "And it's time," he added. He woke up Olive and Persis. It took us all a few minutes to shake the sleep from our foggy brains and understand that now was time for us to escape. Our plan was vague, but we had to try. Rory stood by the entrance to the passageway, peering out. Slung across his back was a sack, which bulged suspiciously. Rolled up in his arms was what seemed to be a rug. I looked at the space it had left on the floor. It was the ugly rug that had supposedly bitten Olive.

Probably a good idea to take something to keep us warm, I thought. It might get cold as we climb down the mountain. But I wasn't so sure about the rest of the stuff.

"Hey, Rory, what's in the sack?" I demanded.

"Stuff," he muttered.

I prodded it. It jangled.

"Are you stealing their treasure?" I asked.

He shuffled his feet and looked everywhere—except at me.

"So what?" he said. "Olive helped out as Cinderella when she did the cleaning at the Inn of the Fluffy Kitten; Persis protected us in Scary Forest with her axe. I'm Ali Baba, so I should do something. And in the story, Ali Baba stole treasure. You never know, we might need to pay for food or something with it. And besides, those goblins owe us."

He had a point. We had been brought up not to steal or lie, but I decided that under these circumstances, one out of two was okay.

"That's all right," I told him. "It's a good idea to take some money and something to keep us warm, too," I added, looking at the carpet he held. Rory gave me a strange look. "And don't worry," I continued, "it's not like I have been any help as Rapunzel."

"Yet," said Persis' voice from behind me. I turned around to look at her. I wasn't sure what she meant, but I was sure I wasn't going to like it. I racked my memory. Just what was it Rapunzel did? Oh, that's right, she let a prince climb up her hair. Well, no princes here, so no-one to climb up my hair. Phew.

I soon discovered that I had "phewed" too soon.

The minute we were all ready to go, Rory peeked down the corridor again.

"All clear," he reported back. "Now follow me, and keep as quiet as you can." All this creeping through caves filled with treasure seemed to be right up his alley. He was silent as a cat, peering around every corner before pressing himself against the wall and sidling along. We did as we were told and followed him out of the entrance to our cave; but instead of turning right, the way we had come, we turned left.

The passageway was short, and it sloped slightly upward. It ended at a rocky wall that had a rough window carved into it. The window had no glass—just like the ones in Tylwyth Teg—so we could feel and smell the fresh air. And we could see that it was the dead of night: a perfect time to escape.

Persis and Rory turned to me.

"OK, Rapunzel," they whispered in unison, smirking at me. "It's time to let down your hair.

CHAPTER 39

"Are you kidding?" I whispered back. I mean, surely it would hurt to have someone climbing down your hair. In fact, it would probably rip the hair out by its roots. Nope, no way was that going to happen to my scalp.

I heard Olive snigger.

"We're not kidding," Persis whispered back. "And we don't have time to argue. But think about it: ever since we got here your hair has grown and grown. There must be a reason for it. Just like there's been a reason for Olive to love cleaning, and for Rory to be a good thief, and for me to love my axe." For a moment, her face clouded with sadness: her precious axe was back in our room in Tylwyth Teg.

I could see what she was getting at. All of our new fairytale characters had added something to this journey, and she was telling me it was my turn. Okay, maybe it was. But there was a flaw in her plan.

"What about me?" I asked. "Say I stand here, and the three of you use my hair to climb down to somewhere flat and safe, where does that leave me? Still here with the goblins and the witch, that's where. And they are not going to be happy when they realize that you three have escaped."

There was a long silence while they thought about this.

"You'll have to climb down your own hair," Olive suggested. She pointed to the stone floor below the window, where a heap of boulders lay. "Tie the end around that and use it to shinny down. When you get to wherever we are, we'll cut your hair off so you can escape— and be rid of your hair at the same time."

It was logical. And we were running out of time. We had to do it. But my poor, beautiful, warm hair! Although the thought of hacking it off made my eyes prickle with tears, she was right. They all were.

Rory pointed to his sack.

"I put a small pair of jeweled nail scissors in here," he said proudly. "We can use that to cut your hair."

That sounded terrible. In fact, everything about it sounded awful. I walked over to the window and climbed onto the highest boulder and peered out. It was too dark to see properly, but I could tell that the drop from the window to the dark mass of trees below was too far to jump without the help of my hair. But if they shinned down to the tip of my hair and then let go, by my reckoning they would only have to drop a couple of feet.

"Okay," I sighed. "Let's do this thing, people." I pulled the twine out of my hair and wished it was stronger so they could use that instead, but when I had searched our cave for something to tie my hair up with, that was all I had found. I leaned over the edge of the window, threw my hair out, and held onto the ledge with all my might.

Rory went first, for two reasons. One, he is my little brother and likes to do anything that might cause me pain or annoyance. Two, he was the lightest. He clambered over my back, 'accidentally' stepped on my face, and then placed his feet on the ledge, at the same level as my head. He gripped my hair with both hands and started to lower himself backward out of the window, using only my hair to keep him from plummeting several meters down to prickly trees and razor-sharp rocks.

CHAPTER 40

Ow. Owww.

OWWWWW!

It hurt quite a bit, but probably not as much as the fuss I was making suggested. I was still going "ow" when Olive (who else?) pointed out that Rory was down and the three tugs on my hair that I felt were him telling me he was on the ground. He had had to drop a short distance, but my hair had reached far enough.

"Oh," I said. She went next, muscling in ahead of Persis. It may have been unkind of me, but I thought her insistence on going next was less to do with being worried about leaving Rory alone and more to do with getting out of the King Azul's mountain lair as soon as she could.

She was a lot heavier than Rory and I silently cursed the witch's high-calorie diet. I closed my eyes and gritted my teeth. The pain was genuine this time, and I concentrated hard on not crying. My nails grated against the rough stone of the wall and began to break. One finger started to bleed but the pain on my head was much, much worse. Several hairs ripped out, roots, skin and all. If this was Olive, I was dreading Persis. Finally, three tugs and my scalp relaxed. I opened my eyes to see Persis' anxious face. There were little tears in the corner of my eyes. Gently she touched my face and wiped away the moisture.

"Are you going to be okay?" she asked. Looking braver than I felt (quite a lot braver to be honest), I nodded.

"Yup, I'll be fine. Just be quick, okay?" I knew she would. She was amazing in gym at school.

"I will," she promised. "And then you get down there with the rest of us as soon as you can."

I didn't need telling twice.

Persis climbed onto the ledge and wiggled her backside so it hung out of the window. She was the biggest and heaviest of all of us, but she was strong and fast. I was praying that this would be quick. She gripped my hair with both hands, whispered a swift, "Sorry," and then her whole weight was on me.

I yelped aloud with shock and from the sting of a handful of hair being ripped from its roots. I almost let go of the ledge as another couple of finger nails snapped off. Then I heard a crashing noise. She had let go early to save me from more agony, and had fallen the rest of the way. The relief on my sore head was wonderful, but it wouldn't last long.

Now it was my turn. I hauled my hair back up, and re-twisted it to form a kind of rope. I found the heaviest boulder I could manage to lift, and forced the tips of my hair underneath it, then let the boulder drop with an echoing bang. If my scream a couple of minutes earlier hadn't alerted the goblins to our escape, surely the noise of the boulder being dropped back would. I had to hurry. I struggled onto the window ledge. That darned pink, ruffled dress was not helping. I turned around, facing up toward the passageway, and copied Persis' backside-first technique. Holding onto my hair-rope, I began to scrabble for a foothold on the outside of the mountain. It wasn't easy going, but I put my toes on small crevices and rocks, and managed to inch down.

Then the boulder holding my hair in place began to move.

CHAPTER 41

I dropped a couple of inches and my feet dangled in the air for a terrifying and painful few seconds, until I managed to grip something with my toes. I was more grateful than ever that I still had my sneakers from the real world with me. I took a few deep breaths to steady myself.

It was okay; I was going to be okay. I didn't look down. I kept all my focus on the sheer rocky drop in front of me and moved down a little more. My breathing and heart rate slowed down to almost normal and I kept moving as fast as I dared. Then I heard Persis yell out to me.

"Brina! Brina! They're coming!" Who were coming? I risked a glance upward and stared straight into the eyes of the Goblin King. A fat drop of drool fell from Azul's mouth, and I could only watch as it descended toward me. It landed right on my forehead.

I could hear scrabbling sounds from below me as my friends clambered up the slope toward me.

"Jump!" Persis shouted. "We'll catch you." No, I couldn't. I'd break my leg and then we'd be in real trouble. Olive and Rory joined in.

"Brina, jump! Jump!" In my panic, I let go and did what they said. I closed my eyes, pushed out with my feet, and leapt.

I felt a yank on my scalp as the boulder stopped my fall but I had a lovely soft landing; I don't think Olive, Rory and Persis enjoyed it as much as I did though. Six hands shoved me up from the tangle of arms and legs, and I staggered back to my feet. Suddenly, I found myself hauled up onto my tiptoes. I shrieked and clutched at my already raw head. Olive spotted him first.

"It's that Goblin King," she breathed. "He's pulling at your hair. He's trying to pull you back up. Quick, Rory, hand me your scissors." Rory reached into his sack and fumbled around.

"Hurry up," I snarled, sobbing from the pain. My scalp felt as though it was going to be pulled away from my head, like Velcro. Persis wrapped her arms around my knees and held me tight, so that I wouldn't be hauled back up the mountain by my hair.

"I can't find them," he whimpered.

Olive shoved him away and grabbed the leather bag, wildly throwing out some of the priceless treasures Rory had collected as she searched for the jeweled nail scissors.

"Yes!" She held them up triumphantly then she ran over to me. She took a hank of hair and began to snip.

Snip, snip, snip. She could only cut a few hairs at a time because the scissors were so tiny.

"Hurry up," I wailed. We were all terrified and Rory was sobbing.

Snip, snip, snip. Persis was keeping watch.

"He's not pulling your hair anymore! He's starting to climb down it!" she shrieked. The pain was even worse. King Azul weighed about the same as the four of us put together times by five. Blood was pouring from wounds on my head where great hanks of hair had been ripped out.

"Guys?" I said, my voice low and trembling. "Guys? I want you to go; just go and leave me. Save yourselves." I knew it was the right thing to say, but part of me hoped and hoped that they would stay right there.

They did. Not one of them even moved a muscle. They didn't even look at each other.

Snip, snip, snip. Then, at last, after a final snip, I lurched forward, freed from the tension that had been pulling me up. I landed on my hands and knees.

"Oh brother," said Persis. I felt my head. Yes, she was right: I was a mess. I could only imagine how terrible I looked. There were bald patches where hair had been torn out, and they were sticky with my blood. Some locks were shoulder length, some were short stubble— but, as if it was teasing me, my sparkling little crown was still firmly in place. For a few seconds, vanity was more important than escape. I grabbed the wide cloth sash that Rory had around his middle and began to wind it around my head like a scarf. I hoped it wouldn't turn to dust, but it was fine. Rory'd magically get another sash, and my need was greater than his.

"Oh brother," Persis repeated. This time I turned to see what she was looking at.

The Goblin King was lying on his back on a ledge, not far from the bottom of the rocky drop; what remained of my hair was clenched in his fist and snaked back up to the tiny window. He must have fallen when the tension from my hair was broken.

"Do you think we killed him?" I asked.

Sadly, we hadn't. Azul lifted an arm and pointed upward; we gazed in the direction he was indicating. Back up at the window were the faces of three goblins and Witchy Wu.

"Nope, but I think we made them all pretty angry," said Olive. "It's time to run."

CHAPTER 42

We scrambled down the rocky slope until we reached the trees and ran into the woods, putting as much distance between us and the goblins as we could. When we were too exhausted to go any further, we skidded to a halt.

"Just a quick break to catch our breath," I told everyone.

"No. No more running," said Rory, trying to keep his wobbly voice calm. Even though they had made running difficult, he had carried his sack with the remaining treasures and his rug with him.

"Look, I know you're tired," I began, but he 'shushed' me and began unrolling the rug.

"Yeah, it will be much easier if you leave that behind," I tried again, but again, he 'shushed' me. Now he flicked the rug out so it lay flat on the ground, right on top of pine cones, branches, and pebbles. His sash had reappeared, and this time I noticed it was a fabulous vivid pink color. I was a little jealous and wondered if he'd complain if I took that one to wear instead.

"No more running," Rory repeated, looking up at me at last.

I looked him over. He was freaking out. He even seemed excited. There was only one explanation, one that I had always suspected from the moment he could speak. My little brother was nuts. I nodded sadly. My fears had been confirmed.

"You're nuts," I told him as gently as I could. "We have to run. They're after us." Stubbornly he shook his head. He bent and lifted a corner of the carpet.

"Touch it," he told Persis and Olive.

"Look, if you have to keep it, I'll help you roll it up—but we have to get going," I said, fear and irritation making my voice sharp.

"NO!" he yelled, stamping his foot. His face was set into a hard expression, and his bottom lip jutted out. He folded his arms; his face turned red. I almost expected to see steam come whistling out of his ears.

"This is not the time for a tantrum," I said, using a tactic that had never, ever worked before.

"NO!" he screamed into my face. "I DON'T WANT TO RUN!" It must have hurt his throat to scream so loudly. He sat down cross-legged, right in the middle of the carpet.

"They can help roll it up," he said. I guess he saw a way to get the others to do what he wanted after all.

Olive and Persis shared a "this kid is a pain, but we better humor him" look and each picked up a corner at one end of the rug, intending to roll it up, Rory and all.

"Yeowch." They jumped back as if they had been zapped. Rory beamed with pleasure. He gestured grandly with his hand.

"This," he announced, "is a flying carpet, which only I can drive."

My opinion hadn't changed. I still thought Rory was nuts.

"We don't have time for your baby games," I snapped. I bent down and grabbed the carpet. It didn't sting me, as it had the others, but it definitely wriggled free from my hand. "What the heck?"

"Did you see that?"

"Huh?"

"I told you so." Why is it that little brothers can be so smug? I opened my mouth to tell him so, but Olive butted in.

"We don't have time for an argument," she said, looking back toward the remains of my hair and the sounds of goblin voices. She took a leap of faith and stepped onto the carpet.

"Huh," she muttered. "It didn't try to bite me this time."

"That's because I want you to climb on, and it listens to me," Rory explained, still smug.

"That's because I want you to climb on, and it listens to me," I mimicked in an unkind baby voice.

Persis flicked a "grow up" look at me and followed Olive's lead. They both sat cross-legged behind Rory. All three twisted around and looked expectantly at me.

I still couldn't take it seriously.

"How did you know it would listen to you?" I demanded.

"While you were snoring your head off, I wondered why it bit Olive, but not me; so I tried it out. When I whispered at it to move, it pretended to be a caterpillar and wriggled across the cave floor," he explained, as if this was a perfectly normal event.

"This is dumb," I said, stepping onto the carpet, in spite of my misgivings. We had approximately thirty seconds to spare before we had to run—and this time, we really had to run. I sat down.

The carpet bucked me off like an irate bronco. I rolled backward with a gasp of surprise and landed on my back, with my legs in the air.

"I don't think my carpet likes you very much," said Rory.

CHAPTER 43

Seriously? Was this kid kidding me? Firstly, there were no such things as flying carpets in real life; and secondly, if there were flying carpets, I was certain they wouldn't be able to pick friends.

As I struggled to my feet, I heard a crash and some words that I assumed were goblin oaths, which meant there were goblins after us—and not too far away.

I grabbed hold of my skirt and started to walk. I was all by myself, being chased by people who wanted to eat me, and I'd probably get caught because of a dumb idea of Rory's. Everything felt like it was too much for me. I was close to tears and felt like having a tantrum myself. I couldn't understand why my friends had turned against me and were sitting on a grubby little rug when goblins were after us. They should have been following me and getting away.

"Please Sabrina," called Persis. "Don't go away; we have to stick together." My face felt all hot. If we had to stick together, then shouldn't they be with me? So far, I was the one who had led them, wasn't I? I looked back at them, and was about to beckon them to follow me, when I saw a rather strange sight.

Rory was kneeling right at the front of the carpet, gripping the fringed edge with both hands. He kept saying "giddy up" while behind him Olive and Persis were holding on for dear life as the rear of the carpet flicked up and down.

Rory turned to me, his face frantic.

"You have to get on, Brina," he said. "It won't go until you're on as well."

Putting aside the strange thought that a temperamental flying carpet was somehow talking to my brother, I said, "So how come it bucked me off then?"

Rory's eyes lost focus for a second then he replied. "Because you were teasing me. Now you should say you're sorry and get back on."

"I see them!" A goblin voice was suddenly very close to us.

"Eep," I squeaked as I jumped right onto the carpet. "I'm sorry, I'm sorry, I'm sorry," I gabbled.

"Giddy up," Rory yelled again.

The goblins were now so close I could smell them. Yuk.

"Maybe it's not 'giddy up'. Maybe it's a magic word?" suggested Persis.

A magic word?

"Open sesame," Rory tried first. Nothing. "Abracadabra!" he screeched next.

The goblins burst through a tangle of branches and leaves that had blocked us from their sight. They stopped still and stared at the sight of four young people sitting in a rug in the middle of the forest.

"Up, up, and away!" Rory hollered.

The carpet gave a lurch and rose a few inches from the ground. That spurred the goblins on. There were two of them, and they both leapt toward us.

I think the carpet might have run on scream-power: the four of us all screamed in unison as the dirty, sharp goblin-claws slashed through the air at us. The carpet seemed to pull slightly in on itself at each corner, like a horse gathering itself for a huge leap, and then it sprang forward and upward.

We kept right on screaming, and hung on to any patch of carpet we could grip. My nails and fingers were already sore as they bit into the fabric, but I was so terrified I didn't notice. The carpet dipped wildly to the left and the right and smashed through twigs and branches which sliced at our skin. Our stomachs dropped down as it went up and then came back up as it unexpectedly dipped low.

"I feeeeellll siiiiiccckkkk," Olive moaned, her words whipped from her mouth as the air rushed past us.

No surprises there, but it was a surprise that the carpet decided to wheel around over the patch we had taken off from. The area was now filled with goblins, including their King, who was shaking his fist up at us.

Olive leaned over the edge of the carpet and threw up, all over the Goblin King. He danced around in fury, waving his fists at us but it gave me a great idea. I grabbed Rory's bag of loot and took a heavy gold goblet out. Aiming carefully, I threw it at King Azul as hard as I could with one hand. He was wiping Olive's sick from his eyes and didn't see it coming. It thunked right onto his crown, and he dropped like a felled tree.

"Hey, Rory, we can use some of your treasure to fight off the goblins," I yelled. So, as Rory struggled to control the flying carpet, Persis, Olive and I each held onto the rug with one hand and threw whatever we could at the goblins with the other. Some missed, but the barrage of glittering gems, coins, and golden objects kept the goblins at bay as we rose higher and higher, out of their reach. Our last sight of them was as they hopped around in fury and tried to wake up their unconscious king. We had definitely not made any friends in our short stay at the goblins' lair.

CHAPTER 44

The journey was horrifying. The flying carpet was almost impossible to steer. Rory did his best, and pulled on the tassels at the left-hand or right-hand corners to change direction. Sometimes he gave a gentle tug on the left and the carpet whirled around and around in an anticlockwise direction. Sometimes he gave a hard yank and the carpet just continued the same way it was already going. Sometimes it flew smoothly at one level, but most of the time it moved up and down as if we were riding a roller coaster. It was stubborn and contrary and mostly did whatever it wanted to. It felt wobbly beneath our weight and we were constantly in danger of falling over the edge. As I got more used to it, I decided that it seemed to be enjoying its freedom from the goblins as well. Whenever we flew over a field of animals, it swooped down leaving our frightened shrieks floating on the air behind us. The magic flying carpet got so excited when it saw a herd of unicorns running through grassland that it followed them for ages, plunging low across their backs then soaring up toward the clouds again as we clung on for dear life, our legs kicking wildly against thin air.

"I think Ruggy's been lonesome," panted Rory at one point. "They must need to be with their—I don't know—their tribe, or something."

Olive took a short break from moaning and dry-retching to agree with him.

"Like horses I expect," she said. Of course. She would be able to afford riding lessons! "Horses are herd animals. When people buy a horse and leave it in a field by itself, it gets lonely. That's why we have a rescue donkey as well as my pony." Of course. She wouldn't just have riding lessons. She would have her own pony as well. I wasn't jealous, much!

"At least Ruggy isn't doing a loop de loop," said Persis. Ruggy? These three had certainly taken the idea that this lump of woven wool was a living thing very seriously.

"Do you think Ruggy knows we are supposed to be heading to that Royal Castle place in Timaru?" I asked. What the heck? Now I was doing it, too.

Rory shrugged his shoulders up and down. I didn't like that. It didn't bode well. "Well?" I pushed. "I mean, how exactly are you talking to, uh, Ruggy?"

"I don't know," Rory said. I furrowed my forehead. "It's not like he's got a voice and I hear words or anything. It's like having a cat or a dog. They look at you or wind around your feet with their bodies if they want you to feed them. They don't use words but you know what they want." Since our cat only ever wanted feeding or letting out—then back in, and then back out—it was usually pretty easy to understand what Mr. Whiskers was trying to tell us.

"Or a horse," chipped in Guess Who. "It's like having a bond with them."

Rory nodded, excited that Olive understood what he was trying to say.

"So does this 'bond' let you know if we're going the right direction?" I asked, fighting hard to keep the sarcasm out of my voice.

Ruggy answered for Rory. He waggled from side to side twice, then rose and sped up, before zooming toward a bluey-gray patch on the horizon.

Now I was calling it "he" instead of "it". Perhaps Ruggy liked it, though, because he stopped messing around and kept at the same level and speed for the rest of our journey. The bluey-gray patch became clearer. It was a large collection of buildings that were a lot like the ones we had seen in Tylwyth Teg but bigger. Some of them seemed to be made of stone and bricks, and some had tiled roofs instead of straw or wood. It was late afternoon by now, and the streets were filled with people and ox carts. There was a well in the center of the town, set in a patch of lush green grass; women and girls were gathered around it, gossiping and laughing. I felt a pang of jealousy at their calm uncomplicated lives.

We cast a shadow as we flew overhead, and one or two glanced up at us, and then looked away as if a magic flying carpet was a perfectly natural thing in the capital city of Dralfynia.

Once more I was reminded that none of us really knew a thing about this strange land, and that it was time for us to find a way to go home.

CHAPTER 45

"There!" I called out, pointing ahead. Rory turned back to look at me, then his gaze followed the direction of my finger. We were heading for what had to be the Royal Castle.

It was a disappointment. In fact, it was a bit of a dump. I had imagined a pink marble castle with silk flags flying from its towers and a moat of clear blue water surrounding it. I had even hoped for windows with glass in them. Instead what greeted us was a pile of gray rocks in the shape of a fairytale castle. Here and there were patches of pale pink. In the past, the gray stone must have been overlaid with a thin layer of marble, but most of it had either worn away or had been chipped off by thieves.

The Royal Castle was roughly square with tall slender towers at the back and squat round towers at the front. The tops of these shorter towers were patrolled by soldiers, women and men in uniform who walked backward and forward and carried tall spears. Their uniform was a long piece of bright blue cloth with a hole in the middle for their heads to pop through and a red belt. I could not imagine what they could be guarding in a place as shabby as this.

Around the base of the castle was a dried-up expanse of stinky mud which had probably been the moat. It didn't look at all promising, and yet somehow we had to get in there, find Bridget, and force her to take us home.

"Land somewhere out of sight," I yelled to Rory. I was pretty sick of this flying carpet, and keen to be able to walk again. He nodded and pulled on the right-hand corner of Ruggy.

Ruggy immediately wheeled to the left and plummeted downward. "Aarrgghh!" I screamed.

"Aarrgghh!" Olive and Persis screamed along with me.

"Woo hoo!" shrieked Rory, circling his fist in the air like a cowboy. Ruggy dumped us onto the grass at the back of the castle, near some deep pits which smelled a lot worse than the Melas town dump on a hot day. These pits seemed to be covered in a gray layer of furry mould. Above us, seagulls and crows cawed and circled, and flies buzzed everywhere.

"Oh great. Ruggy's brought us to the middens," Olive squeaked, her fingers tight on her nose. She looked very pale. The journey had been worst for her.

"Middens?" Persis asked. Olive nodded.

"In the olden days, there would be middens behind houses, or just outside towns, and they were where the people used to get rid of their waste, like old food, and, um … well, they didn't have flushing toilets, so … you get the picture."

We all took several steps backward.

Ruggy wriggled after us. He was back in his caterpillar mode.

"That explains a lot," said Persis, looking unexpectedly pleased. Seeing the looks of puzzlement in our faces, she continued. "Whenever my room at home is a mess, my mom tells me to tidy up my 'midden.' Whenever I ask her what it is, she tells me to look it up so I'll remember it. And now I don't have to," she finished triumphantly.

"There's someone coming," I hissed. "Quick, hide." I had seen a small wooden door open at the base of the castle. A woman in a plain black dress with a white apron came out. We scurried to a convenient heap of boulders. We ducked down, and then one by one peeped over the top to watch her. She carried a wooden pail over the nearest pit and threw the contents onto it.

The layer of gray fur parted, and began to churn. It wasn't a layer of furry mould—it was a layer of rats, which were now fighting over food scraps.

CHAPTER 46

I gulped back a terrified whimper and started to shake from head to toe and here's why. When I was three, Dad had taken me to visit a petting zoo, one of those places where little kids get to stroke baby goats and sheep. The people there had let me put a scoop into a big sack of feed to give to the chicks. I had reached right into the bag with my little scoop as far as I could, armpit deep and wondered why it felt kind of hairy. I looked down and saw not one but several pairs of eyes looking back up at me. Then a family of rats which had been feasting in the bag used my arm, shoulder and head as a bridge on their way out. Even now I can feel their little claws skittering up my bare arms. Ever since then, I have had a morbid fear of rats and, if you ask me, it's totally justified.

So, now we needed a way into the castle that didn't involve going within ten miles of the rat mat. I pushed the rats from my mind, almost anyway, and began to plan. I pinched my lower lip as I thought. We were so close to finally getting back home and I wanted to get this right.

"We have a couple of ways in, I think," I whispered to the others. "We could just go to the front door and ask for Bridget." They all looked skeptical.

"If Aidan was right, we don't know who we can trust," Persis pointed out. "I mean any of those soldiers or servants would probably tell the Beast with Nine Fingers we were looking for Bridget. For all we know, the prince could even be right here, visiting his aunt. Don't forget what Aidan, said," she reminded me.

"So ...?" I wasn't sure what she meant.

"So if we all turn up and ask for someone who has a price on her head, people might capture us to get to her so they can get the reward."

"Right, that's true. The direct approach is out, then." I thought some more. "I guess the only other option is to jump on Ruggy again and get him to take us up there," I continued, pointing up to the towers. Right away, as if they could hear me, three soldiers walked to the edge of the tower and peered over, then took it in turns to pitch apple cores into one of the pits. I could faintly hear the squeaks of the happy rats.

"I've got a better idea," Olive announced.

Not "another idea", but an actual "better" one. I frowned, but she kept talking.

"We need to sneak in. And I think that if we all go in, we could draw too much attention to ourselves. I think the best thing is if one of us sneaks in, finds your stepmom and brings her back here to the rest of us."

Hmm, not a bad idea, I thought. How annoying.

"All right," I said, getting to my feet. "That makes sense, Olive. Well done," I added, just to make sure she knew I was still the boss of our gang, in Dralfynia anyway. But she was shaking her head and pulling me down again.

"No, not you. I mean, look at you. Look at your hair; it's already grown another two or three inches." She reached up and pulled the scarf from my head. I ran my hand over my skull. She was right. The wounds had scabbed and soft baby hairs had grown over the bald patches. She continued, "You're instantly recognizable as one of the kids being chased by the Goblin King. You would stand out as soon as you set foot in the Royal Castle."

Well, if not me—then who? I looked at Persis in her red hood and cloak, and Rory in his shiny outfit. There really was no choice. It had to be Olive.

She read my mind and nodded.

"I already look like a servant. I can sneak in that door there, by the middens, and no one will even give me a second glance."

She was right but I didn't want to give up without a fight.

"But you've never met Bridget," I objected. "How will you recognize her? And how will you persuade her to come out here?"

"You'll have to describe her for me," Olive replied. "I already know she has one blue eye and one brown eye. And if she's on the same side as Aidan is on, I'm sure she'd want to help her step-kids get back home."

While Rory was using the words 'brown hair,' 'short,' and 'plump' to describe Bridget, I was trying to make sense of Olive's comment about Aidan.

She had been listening to what he said. I suspected that she had noticed his freckles and dimples, too.

CHAPTER 47

The last we saw of Olive as we hid behind our rocks, was the sight of her sauntering confidently toward the small wooden door. We saw her bend down and pick up an empty wooden pail that had been dumped there, and then she pulled open the door, ducked her head and walked straight in. She didn't even look back at us to wave goodbye.

"She's so brave," Rory breathed. "I'd be too scared to go in there all by myself," he added.

"Yeah, me too," I confessed. We settled down to wait. And wait. And wait. Evening began to fall. It got darker, and we started to get hungry and cold.

Luckily, we were spotted by some of the guards on the tower, captured, and thrown into a dungeon before I had to sit out there in the pitch dark, with hundreds of rats nearby. But more of that later.

CHAPTER 48

Olive hoped she looked natural as she lifted up the heavy wooden bucket by its rough rope handle. Inside her head she hummed her favorite songs as she went along, just to give her something to think about. She didn't dare sing it aloud though, as she didn't think the people in Dralfynia knew about hip-hop and rap.

Although singing to herself made her look confident, inside she was shaking. She knew the others were relying on her, and she was desperate to get back home. She had felt like the outsider in the group ever since this insane adventure had begun, and she wanted to be back with her family. And of course, she was afraid that she would get caught. What if they tortured her to get her to tell where the others were? She was pretty certain she would give in right away—she usually made a huge fuss if she got so much as a splinter. As she entered a vast steam-filled kitchen, she gave a little shudder at the thought.

"What's up with you, my girl?" yelled a huge, red-faced woman. She stood by a roaring fire which had an enormous stew pot hanging above it. She wielded a wooden spoon, which was dripping with a rich, dark sauce. Olive's stomach rumbled as she stared at the spoon, desperate to taste it, but no-one heard it over the noise of shouting and banging that filled the room.

Olive looked around her, wondering what girl the woman was talking to.

"If you're shiverin,' you come 'ere and stir this pot," the woman continued to yell.

Oh, the woman was talking to her.

"Um, it's all right, thank you very much," Olive said. "I, um, I have to go and get some parsnips. I thought they would make a nice change from pumpkins." The kitchen fell silent as everyone turned to look at her.

"A change from pumpkins?" quavered an old crone who was making pumpkin scones. Her mouth had dropped open in her shock, showing absolutely no teeth at all.

"Oh, uh ... ha, ha. I was just joking, of course. I mean, I am just going to get some ..." Olive had almost no knowledge of vegetables and cooking. Her mind went blank, but as she mentally groped around for a reason to leave this hellish room, a door was flung wide open and another young girl staggered in carrying a plank of wood across her shoulders. From each end of the plank dangled a wooden pail, slopping full of water.

"... water!" Olive cried in relief. "I have to go get some water. Of course I do, what was I thinking when I said parsnips, ha ha. So anyway, lovely to meet you. Bye bye." She shot out through the doorway into a blessedly cool, stone-walled corridor, leaving behind a kitchen filled with puzzled faces and the buzzing noise of a dozen people all repeating the word 'parsnips' over and over.

She skittered along the corridor as fast as she could, keen to put some distance between her and the other servants. The passageway was wide with a smooth stone floor covered in mats made from woven rushes which tickled her bare feet. Although the cool flagstones were more soothing to her sore feet, she kept to the mats, trying to deaden the sound of her footsteps as she ran.

The Royal Castle was like a maze with twists and turns and unexpected staircases. Olive assumed that as a witch and here to visit the duchess, Bridget Bishop Summers would not be down in the servants' area of the castle, so whenever she came across a staircase, she made the decision to go up. The first staircase spiraled around and around, while the stairs themselves got narrower and steeper. It was hard work. Panting, she finally reached a wooden door set into a deep, stone wall.

Cautiously, she pushed it open a few inches and peeped through, straight into the face of one of the soldiers patrolling the top of a tower.

"Oopsy, wrong tower," she said, pulled the door closed, and ran back down the twisting stairs as fast as she could. Only when she had reached the bottom did she dare to pause and look back up. As far as she could tell, the door had not reopened, and she was safe to catch her breath.

Her approach of wandering aimlessly around and hoping to bump into someone she had never met before was not working. Olive needed a plan. She pulled a rag from her skirt pocket and polished a few door knobs as she thought.

"If I was a librarian witch from Massachusetts, but I was now in a Royal Castle in Dralfynia, where would I be?" she mused aloud. Then she clicked her fingers. "Ah, the library, that's where I would be," she decided, a smile brightening her dirt-smeared face.

"Can I help you at all, Miss?" said a very tiny, but sarcastic voice by her feet. Olive looked down and almost laughed out loud. A tall mouse dressed in a purple velvet coat and standing on her hind legs was looking up at her.

CHAPTER 49

"Did you say something?" Olive asked, feeling very glad that Sabrina wasn't there to see her talking to a mouse.

"Yes, I asked if you needed some help. You are a long way from the servants' quarters, you know," the mouse repeated. She was quite a cute thing with bright black eyes and white whiskers that trembled when she spoke. Well, maybe this wasn't so strange after all. In the fairy story, Cinderella had been helped by the mice that became her footmen, so perhaps this mouse could help her.

Of course, if there had been any chance that the fairy story was going to come true, someone would have magicked her a beautiful gown and coach by now, and she would have been given an invitation to the ball, instead of having to sneak in the servants' door at the back of the castle. Still, she didn't have a lot of choice.

"Yes please, um, Mrs. Mouse. I would like to go to the library. Can you take me there?"

"Servants like you aren't allowed in the library," said the mouse huffily.

It was time for more servant-type fibs.

"I was sent for ... to ... um ... to clean up the cinders in the hearth," Olive said, almost quoting word for word from the big book of fairy stories she had read when she was a little girl.

The mouse looked her up and down, and apparently decided that Olive did look like someone who would clean out fireplaces. She pointed her tiny paw to the right.

"Follow the corridor. Take the first staircase you come to. When you come to a carpeted corridor, turn right. The library is behind the double doors at the end. Make sure none of the nobles catch sight of you. They don't like to see the servants."

Olive thanked the mouse and then bobbed a curtsey. She had definitely been playing the part of Cinderella for far too long; she needed to get her old, feisty character back.

It was an uncomfortable feeling to have a large mouse stand on its hind feet and watch her until she disappeared from sight. She hoped Mrs. Mouse wouldn't tell anyone she'd seen her.

She followed the mouse's directions until she came to a corridor, paneled on each side with wood that she was dying to polish, and had a thick carpet on the ground that she dearly wanted to sweep.

She almost cried with pleasure at the feeling of soft wool beneath her feet and stopped still, rocking backward and forward just to feel the carpet squishing between her toes. It was bliss. She closed her eyes and let herself have the luxury of a few moments of simple comfort and peace. With a sigh she then gave herself a little mental shake and opened her eyes. At the end of a corridor was a double door covered in peeling paint. Suddenly a tiny panel in one door slid open and a blue eye peeped out at her. Olive stared and gave a nervous wave. Then both doors were flung wide open and in the doorway stood a woman, staring at her suspiciously. She looked beyond Olive, checking out the corridor and then back at the girl.

Their eyes met. Olive's were green. The woman looking at her had one blue eye and one brown. Finally, after all the adventures and drama, she had found Bridget.

"Oh boy, am I glad to see you," Olive cried, and rushed to fling her grimy arms around the woman.

"Excuse me?" the woman said, taking a large step back. "Just exactly why is one of the servants so happy to see me? No-one is supposed to know I'm here." Olive stopped in her tracks, suddenly aware of how this must look to the woman who she hoped was her ticket back home.

"Are you Bridget Bishop?" she asked, feeling awkward and shy. "I mean, Bridget Bishop Summers?"

The woman's jaw dropped open in shock.

"No one here calls me that," she whispered. "Just who are you, and where are you from?"

CHAPTER 50

Half an hour later, Olive found herself sitting in a very comfortable padded chair in a room filled with books, globes, paintings, mirrors, and tables covered with maps, charts and crystals. She sipped a cup of tea and stretched her grubby toes toward a small fire. She nibbled a little piece of delicious sponge cake and sighed happily.

The little mouse had been summoned by Bridget to bring refreshments. Being a guest of the duchess meant Bridget had some protection it seemed. Olive approved—Mrs. Mouse had not been happy to wait on someone who looked like the lowest of all the servants.

Bridget was far less peaceful. She strode about the room, repeating back to Olive the story she had told her, trying to make sense of it all.

"And where did you say Clyde was?" she demanded. She seemed more worried about Clyde than the rest of them. Olive explained again that Clyde had been stabled at the Inn of the Fluffy Kitten when the rest of them had been kidnapped by the goblins. Bridget thought for a moment.

"Aidan will have freed him and he'll be on his way here," she said.

"Who will be on his way? Aidan?" Olive asked, a lilt of hope in her voice.

"What? No, Clyde. He knew you were coming here. He knows the way. He'll be fine."

That puzzled Olive. They had all assumed that Clyde was there by accident, like the rest of them.

"So Clyde's been to Dralfynia before then?" she asked. She was starting to be as suspicious of this witch as Sabrina had been.

Bridget stared at her, trying to decide what to say.

Olive read her uncertainty in her face.

"Please just tell me the truth. I deserve that much after everything I've been through," she said, sweeping her hand along her ragged outfit.

Bridget nodded slowly.

"You're right, you do. When I recognized Clyde in the field in Melas, I adopted him as my witch's familiar."

Olive's eyes bugged out.

"Aren't they creatures that help witches? And aren't they usually cats or owls?" Bridget blushed.

"Well, yes they are. But Clyde was so lovely, and I was so excited at finding someone from home in your land." She gave a little shrug. "And I just couldn't resist his big brown eyes. So now we help each other and I bring him back home to visit as often as possible." Olive tried to make sense of this but had more questions than answers. Clyde had been in Melas first—how had he got there? Why was he there? Why hadn't he stayed in Dralfynia when Bridget had brought him back?

Bridget had returned to her pacing around the library and interrupted Olive's thoughts. "Now tell me, exactly how did you all get here after you escaped from the goblins?"

"Oh, we came here on Ruggy," said Olive through a mouthful of cookie. She had pushed aside any feelings of guilt about the others waiting outside in the cold with no food pretty quickly.

"Ruggy?"

"Oh that's what we call the magic flying carpet. He was kind of a pain because he kept biting Persis and me, and although he was OK with Sabrina in the end, he only listened to Rory. He was pretty uncooperative," she added, remembering the horrible journey she had suffered as a result of Ruggy's whims.

Bridget stopped and stood stock still. She stared at Olive with her mouth hanging open. "A flying carpet?" she repeated, her voice faint.

Olive nodded.

"A magic flying carpet that had been captured by the goblins?"

Olive nodded again.

"That's right. Though it would only let Rory fly it. It was kind of mulish."

Bridget hurried across to Olive and gripped her arm.

"Describe it to me," she demanded.

Olive did her best, though Ruggy's complicated pattern was hard to explain. Her words satisfied Bridget though.

Bridget dropped Olive's arm, her expression thoughtful. "It must be the one, but only the royals can—" she caught herself, looked at Olive, and snapped her mouth shut.

Olive looked at her, waiting for her to finish her sentence, but Bridget changed the subject.

"Listen Olive, you kids are in terrible danger."

That caught Olive's attention.

"Danger? Like from the Beast with Nine Fingers you mean?"

If Bridget was surprised that Olive knew about the prince's nickname, she didn't show it. "Yes, from him, and from all those who follow him. If he finds out you know me and you're from a different world, he will have you killed. He sees anyone who is different as a threat," said Bridget.

Olive wasn't sure that Bridget was being totally honest and her incomplete sentence hung in the air, but from her point of view the faster they all got home, the better.

It seemed as if Bridget had read her mind. She turned to the bookshelves and spoke over her shoulder to Olive. "We need to get you all back home—and as soon as possible," she said. "I'm going to show you the spell you need, then it's up to you to get the others and cast the spell by the well in the middle of Timaru."

Olive nodded. She remembered flying over it on Ruggy.

Bridget explained more. "The well is like the horse trough in the field in Melas. The water acts as a portal, or door, between the two lands. With any luck, you'll be back home in time for dinner."

Bridget's expression softened as she looked at Olive. "You poor things. You must have been terrified."

Olive didn't like to admit it. She lifted one shoulder and let it drop casually, hoping that the witch would think she was cool.

"Don't worry, dear. It's all going to be fine. Your parents won't even have had time to notice you've been gone."

Olive stared at her.

"How can that be? We've been here for days," she pointed out.

"It's complicated," said Bridget, carefully. "Dralfynian time moves at a different pace.

People prefer a slower pace of life here, and although it means they are a bit behind the times, they like it that way. This whole kingdom is like that." She glanced at Olive. "How are you feeling?" she asked suddenly. "Sometimes moving between the realms can make humans feel unwell."

Olive shook her head.

"No, I feel fine," she told her. Privately, Olive thought a few modern conveniences would make a great difference to Dralfynia and perhaps it should start keeping up with the real world.

Bridget clapped her hands firmly, and said "Right!" in the manner that adults use when they want kids to get up and do stuff.

Olive crammed the last of the treats into her mouth, brushed the crumbs off her clothes and into the fire, and waited to be told what to do next.

Bridget hurried around the room, pulling books from shelves and muttering "Now where is it ..." until finally she said "Ah ha!"

She pulled an enormous book from a high shelf, and tottered around comically beneath its weight. It was brown with gold lettering, and held hundreds of pages of thick, dry paper, which were speckled with brown age spots. Bridget dumped it on a table and sneezed twice as dust flew from it. She flung it open, ignoring the painful creak it gave as its spine cracked, and her fingers flew through the pages like a whirlwind.

"Ah ha," she repeated, and jabbed her finger down on a page. "This is the spell we need. Now, you copy it out, I just need to warm up the magic mirror so we can make sure the others are okay." Bridget went to the far end of the room, where a tall object covered with a cloth was set in an alcove. She ripped the covering off stood before a wooden-framed mirror and began to rub dust from the glass. Olive thought she heard the mirror giggle.

Olive looked around her. All she could see was thick parchment paper and feathers. No notepads or pens. It would have been much easier if she'd had her smartphone with her. She could have just taken a photo of the spell and carried that with her. No chance that anything at all in this land would be as easy as that. Instead, she took up one of the feathers, and dipped the pointy end into a glass bottle of what she assumed was ink. She placed it onto a piece of the parchment and dragged the tip across the page. Leaving little tears and big blobs of ink along the way, she copied the spell onto the parchment as carefully as she could.

CHAPTER 51

Spell to Return to One's Own Realm

A magic item there must be,
In the hand of each of ye.
One may carry what's brown and sticky,
Even though it may be icky.
Another the hair from a magic horse,
Be sure to ask his permission of course.
A third a comforting item will take,
The warmest thing a cat can make.
Finally, wood chopped by the hand
Of the woodsman's daughter, and
Set all aflame and say this rhyme:
"Back to my home and back to my time."
Say it thrice while holding tight
To friends and family with all thy might.
Close thy eyes and count to three,
Open them and you will see,
Exactly where thou wants to be.

Olive had no idea what any of this meant, but she felt better knowing Bridget was there to help them. She blew on to the messy page, smearing some more of the ink around and then looked over at Bridget.

Bridget was arguing with the magic mirror.

"Look, you just need to show me where they are," she said, annoyed.

"Oh Bridg, don't be so bossy. You'll get wrinkles," came from the direction of the mirror.

Bridget curled her hands into fists, put them on her hips and stamped her feet.

"Look, Meera, stop being silly. You know who I'm trying to help here, don't you? Just do what you're told," she said.

Olive looked up to watch. There was the outline of a face in the mirror and it seemed to be pouting.

Next, Bridget tried pleading.

"Please can you just show me her kids are OK? Please? Pretty please?"

The mirror was silent.

She tried flattery. "Look, there are other mirrors, you know, but none of them are as good as you are. You're the best of all." She dropped her voice almost to a purr.

Olive wasn't sure, but she thought the glass in the mirror turned a little pink.

"Oh Bridg," said the mirror, "you know you can always sweet talk me around. Go on then, here they are."

Olive walked over to join Bridget, folding her parchment now that the ink was dry, and stuffed it into one of her patchwork pockets. She gazed, her mouth dropping open, as the mirror no longer reflected the images of herself and Bridget, but showed instead a swirling, sparkling, gray and purple mist. Slowly it began to eddy, going faster and faster. Olive noticed the scent of burning. It was like the smell of the candles on a birthday cake when they have just been blown out. There was a high-pitched whining sound, too, which made her put her hands to her ears because it tickled them deep inside her head. Then there was a little pop, and the mist cleared away.

"That took, like, forever," complained the mirror. "You said they were outside, but when I went to look for them, they weren't there. I had to follow the trail of magic that the flying carpet left behind to find them."

"Thanks, Meera, you did a great job," Bridget said, but the image that they saw made her voice flat.

"I know," was the smug reply.

Bridget and Olive stared with dismay at the vision the mirror was showing them.

Oh no, not again. The others were in another dungeon. Someone else had captured them.

Sabrina and Persis were slumped down against the wall, next to one another. At least they were together. Olive felt a little pang of jealousy. It must make tough times a lot easier if you had a friend to share them with. Rory lay on the floor. He had rolled himself up in his beloved carpet, and looked like a sausage roll.

Bridget gasped at what she saw. She raised a finger and pointed right at Rory, but it wasn't him she was looking at.

"That's it," she said softly. "That's the carpet; after all these years." She rubbed the back of her neck, thinking hard.

"Now, if they're in the dungeon, that means someone working for the Beast has them. And it's only a matter of time before he hears about the carpet and comes to seize it. We've got to rescue them, and we've got to get the carpet away as well." She turned to face Olive again. "Come on, we've got a lot to do."

CHAPTER 52

I was getting pretty sick of being captured and sitting in cold, damp, uncomfortable dungeons. We had been sitting behind our rocks, minding our own business and doing no harm to anyone. I had been complaining about how long Olive was taking; Rory was taking a nap; and Persis was prowling around, looking for a replacement axe. We hadn't noticed that the soldiers on top of the tower had spotted us, and we hadn't noticed the other soldiers sneaking up on us. The first we knew about it was when strong hands gripped hold of us, digging into our arms and legs, and we were flung over the backs of some men in the same tunic uniforms as all the other guards. We screamed and struggled and kicked at their backs, but it was pointless—and it used up too much energy. In the end we just flopped, and waited for the inevitable. We were getting used to being captured and now here we were in yet another dungeon.

"This time, we have to be careful about what we eat and drink," I said, remembering how the golden liquid in our last prison had put us all to sleep. Persis laid her head on my shoulder and sighed.

"I'm so hungry and thirsty, I don't think I would care," she said.

Rory was sulking. He had said, "It's not fair," about three hundred times in a row, without pausing for breath. Then he had rolled himself up in Ruggy and closed his eyes. He hadn't spoken or moved since then, and we had already been there for a couple of hours at least.

Persis was always a girl for action. She stood up and went to the wooden door. It was locked. There was a small window cut into it with iron bars across it. She peered through and then yelled out to the guard who stood on the other side.

"Hey, mister. We're hungry. You're going to be in trouble if we all starve to death you know."

"You wouldn't be the first and you won't be the last," was all the reply we got from the soldier.

"Nice try," I told Persis, trying to comfort her.

"I wonder how Olive's getting on," said Rory from his sulking position.

"Oh her," I said. "She's probably found some guy to suck up to, and he's probably feeding her grapes or something right now. You know what she's like. There's a reason she doesn't have any friends. She's just dumped us. Either that or she's met Bridget and neither of them care about us."

"Well, maybe," Persis said, her voice quiet. "Or ... you know ... maybe something happened to her?"

"If something had happened to her, she'd be in here with us," I pointed out.

We slid back into our gloomy silence. There was nothing we could do but wait.

A few minutes later, we heard footsteps outside our prison door and a different voice. A girl's voice.

"Hey there, Mr. Soldier. How's your day going?"

"Well, young miss, not so bad thanks for your polite consideration, but better now for smelling that food tray of yours. I hope that's for me and not for those prisoners?"

"Oh sir, this food and drink is for the prisoners, I'm afraid. Orders of the Duchess. You know what an old softy she is," said the girl's voice. "Here, do you want a bread roll? They'll never miss one."

There was some chuckling, then a loud thunk—followed by the sound of a soldier falling to the ground.

"Yeah, you can have one of these cast-iron bread rolls right on your dumb head," the girl continued.

There was some jingling while Olive, whose voice I had finally recognized, struggled to find the correct key and unlock the door. She kicked it open, and stood there, in all her grubby glory with a triumphant smile on her face.

"Hey, losers," she announced. "It's time to get out of here."

Finally! It was about time we got rescued. We stumbled out of the dungeon and, pausing only to grab the real bread rolls and a slurp of water from the jug, we followed Olive as she led the way.

"Psst," hissed Persis at me. "Got anything to say about Olive now?"

No. No I didn't have anything to say about Olive now, but in the darkness of the corridor I blushed. However, I did have two questions: why were we following a mouse in a velvet coat? And why was Olive carefully carrying a dirty wooden spoon?

CHAPTER 53

We all stared at the piece of parchment Olive was holding up.

"You need to work on your handwriting," I commented. "It's really hard to read."

I saw the expression in Olive's eyes harden.

"It's difficult to write with a quill and ink," she said. "Especially when you've been dumped in some weirdo world and you're busy rescuing people."

I can't think what made her so touchy.

"So, read it out loud again and let's think this through," I told her. We were standing in a small room, which was carpeted from wall to wall. The room contained a desk covered in parchments, and a chair; there were some pretty tapestries on the walls, and there was even a fire, although it was starting to die down.

We had followed Olive—who, in turn, had followed the mouse—along a complicated route, which took us along passageways, and up and down staircases.

When the mouse in the purple velvet coat left, it hissed unpleasantly at Olive.

To my amazement, she hissed right back. Being in Dralfynia was affecting her fake good manners, I thought.

"Before you read out the spell, Olive," Persis interrupted, "I still don't understand about the trained mouse."

Olive smirked. "I don't think she'd appreciate being called a 'trained mouse' to be honest. She's a senior housekeeper. Like I said ... uh ... she found me in the library when I was copying out the spell that I happened to find there."

"And she just offered to help?" Persis persisted.

"Yep, she just offered to help. I guess some people in Dralfynia are good guys, like Aidan, right?"

Aidan? What was she doing talking about Aidan? He was nothing to do with her.

My dad says that people choose how they react and behave, and I know that "I couldn't help myself" is just an excuse, but this time, I felt as though I really couldn't help myself. It seemed to me that Olive had been needling at me for the whole of our adventure in Dralfynia. She wasn't even part of the group—she had just been in the wrong place at the wrong time, as she had just reminded me. She had pushed in with her ideas, she had been a show-off about her horse—sorry, horse and donkey, she had waited ages to come and rescue us, and now she was flirting with Aidan even though he wasn't here to know it. And who knew what she'd been up to while we were in the dungeon? She was the same at school too, always showing up in the fanciest clothes and coming top in the pop quizzes.

"How would you know what a 'good guy' was?" I said. Olive's perfect and pretty forehead wrinkled as she thought about my remark.

"Are you calling me a 'bad guy'?" she asked, in a quiet voice. "I mean ... are you calling me a bad person?"

Uh oh.

"Well, not exactly," I floundered, briefly wishing I could eat my words. Then I built up momentum. "But you are always showing off that your dad's so rich and that you can afford all those designer clothes. And you show off in class about knowing all the answers, too. Plus, you're so mean. It's no wonder you don't have any friends."

When I decide to pick an unnecessary fight at a time when we should all be pulling together, with someone who basically just saved our lives, I like to do it in style.

Olive gasped.

Persis and Rory held their breath in awe. I don't often lose my temper, so this was a rare sight for them.

Olive called me a bad name. Persis and Rory inhaled even more. I told her she was even more of the same bad name than I was. Persis and Rory were starting to go purple.

"And anyway, what about you?" Olive demanded. "You swan around school with your friends stuck to you—all because you're too scared to stand on your own two feet. And you laugh at me behind my back, just because I'm not the same as you. I may be clever, but it doesn't mean it doesn't hurt my feelings when you call me 'Ayres and Graces,' you know." There were tears in her eyes. "If someone bullied Rory for having red hair, you would stick up for him; but you lead everyone in picking on me because my parents are rich and because I'm not dumb."

"Oh poor you," I sneered. "You have everything handed to you on a plate. You've never had to go to school and then go home and clean the house and look after your little brother, because your mom ran off and then died."

"Yeah, well, you've never had to force yourself to go to school even though you know that you'll sit alone at recess, that you'll never be picked for a sports team, and that you'll be totally ignored every time you try to talk to someone."

There was a very long and very heavy silence. Rory breathed out at last. Everyone waited for one of us to recognize the truth of what the other had said. But we didn't.

In the end, Persis spoke. "Okay then. Moving on, let's have a look at the spell and do something about getting out of here."

CHAPTER 54

Olive flung the piece of paper at Persis, who was doing a pretty good job of pretending nothing had happened. I could see Persis' hands trembling as she took it and her voice quavered as she read the spell aloud. I guess the argument between Olive and me had shocked her and Rory as much as it shocked the two of us.

I knew that I felt ashamed of what I had done, but I didn't like the feeling, so I ignored it. I decided that it was her fault anyway. If she'd come and got us from the dungeon sooner, I wouldn't be so tired and scared, and we'd probably be home by now.

Persis didn't meet either Olive's eyes or mine as she read aloud.

"Okay, so this is a spell to return us to our own realm, which means back to Melas." She cleared her throat and chanted the spell aloud, making suggestions as she went.

"'A magic item there must be, in the hand of each of ye'." She looked up. "I think that means we all need to be have a special object, which we throw on the fire. We have to work out what the special objects are from the rest of the poem. Everyone agree?"

Olive nodded. "That's what uh, I think too." Her voice was so quiet that she was almost whispering.

Persis ploughed on.

"And we all need to be by the well in the center of Timaru, because the water acts like a gate or something when we cast the spell. Okay then." She sighed and took a deep breath as she read through the parchment. "The first one is, 'One may carry what's brown and sticky, even though it may be icky'."

Rory laughed. Before he could tell us what he thought was brown and sticky, Olive held up her wooden spoon.

"I have that right here," she said, still subdued. "I saw it in the kitchen, being used to stir a big pot of something gross. I sneaked back in and got it after I read the spell."

"Well done, Olive," said Persis with rather too much enthusiasm. "Okay, the next part says: 'Another the hair from a magic horse, be sure to ask his permission of course.' Any ideas?"

Rory spoke up. "It sounds like the hair from Clyde's tail or mane or something to me," he said.

Olive was nodding.

"According to Brid—I mean Mrs. Mouse, Clyde made his way to Timaru after we were all kidnapped, and he'll be in a paddock down by the middens. We probably weren't that far from him." Getting Clyde and grooming his tail and mane sounded like the easiest option to me, but Rory had his hand in the air right away, whole seconds before I could even react.

"I'll find him," he volunteered. "And I'll bring him to our meeting place," he added. "I bet he'd like to come home with us."

Persis continued to read.

"A third a comforting item will take, the warmest thing a cat can make. Finally, wood chopped by the hand of the woodsman's daughter." She stared me in the eyes. "Brina, the wood chopping has to be my job, don't you think?"

I nodded without replying. I was too busy trying to think of what my part of the spell meant. The warmest thing a cat can make? I had no idea.

Out of the corner of my eye I saw Olive bend down and whisper to Rory.

He nodded and spoke up. "Brina, I think the warmest thing a cat can make means one of those blankets at the Inn of the Fluffy Kitten."

Of course, it was easy when he pointed it out. "Yes, I think so too, Rory. I was just going to say that," I fibbed. "But how would I get to Tylwyth Teg and back again?" The thought of seeing Aidan was in direct competition with my dread of having to go anywhere near the goblins' mountain, and a long journey on foot.

Again, I saw Olive bend down and whisper in his ear, and again he spoke up. It was obvious that she was telling him what to say because she didn't want me to put her down for showing off again. That feeling of shame from earlier poked me in the tummy.

"Take the flying carpet. It's easy. I'll show you how to ride Ruggy, and you'll be there and back in two or three hours."

I felt a bit scared at the thought of it, but it made sense. And, like I said, I was keen to see Aidan again.

CHAPTER 55

Persis continued to read the rest of the spell:

"Set all aflame and say this rhyme:
'Back to my home and back to my time.'
Say it thrice while holding tight
To friends and family with all thy might.
Close your eyes and count to three,
Open them and you will see,
Exactly where thou wants to be."

She refolded the piece of paper and handed it to Olive. Not to me, I noticed.

"Okay then," she said. "I'll go and find a new axe and cut some wood. Olive, you go and make sure that the area by the well is safe, and wait for the rest of us there." Olive nodded, then turned and left without saying a word. It was a good job she had already explained how we could sneak back out of the castle again; she sure wasn't going to stay around me any longer than she had to.

"As for you two," Persis continued, "Rory, you go and get Clyde—and take the carpet with you; Brina, you go with him, then he can show you how to drive it. I'll see you all down by the well, okay?"

We nodded. I think we were all afraid of being alone, but if we wanted to get home as soon as possible, we had no choice.

Just as Persis started to leave, she stopped and spoke to me over her shoulder. "Just one more thing," she began.

Oh no, I knew what was coming. That's the trouble with a really good friend. They aren't afraid to be truthful with you.

"Brina, you were really mean to Olive just now. I know she's kind of a pain, and I know she was mean right back, but I think you need to sort it out."

Yeah, I thought so too. But not just yet. We watched until Persis' crimson cape fluttered around a corner and she had vanished from sight. I decided to get a second opinion. "Rory, do you think I was—"

"Ohhhh yes," he said. "Come on, I want to see Clyde again." Carrying the rolled-up carpet between us, we crept out of the room. We followed Olive's directions and saw no one the whole way. Within five minutes, we were back outside and scurrying as fast as we could past the middens with their heaving rug of rats, and to some fields beyond. In one was a dear familiar sight. Clyde was grazing among the buttercups and daisies and lush grass, looking fit and well. And best of all, there wasn't an apple in sight.

Rory dropped his end of the carpet, and sprinted toward Clyde as fast as his curling slippers would allow him. He flung his little arms around Clyde's great neck while the horse shook his head and whinnied.

I felt a tear of relief drip from my eye. Thank goodness he was safe. Surely we would all be home in just a few hours. I dragged the carpet along and dropped it to the ground as I joined them so I could hug Clyde as well.

"Hey," Rory said crossly. "Don't drop Ruggy like that. He won't like it," he told me, kneeling down and stroking the carpet. I considered pointing out that he had dumped his end of Ruggy just two minutes earlier, but I decided that it was more important to get on with my task.

"Okay, I'm sorry. I'll be more gentle with Ruggy from now on," I muttered. "Just show me what to do, then you take Clyde down to the well and wait with Olive." Rory unrolled Ruggy with a flourish, and gestured with his arm for me to sit on Ruggy, near the front.

"It seemed to work when I said 'Up, up and away'," Rory began. As soon as the words left his mouth, Ruggy curled in on himself, and then sprang forward and upward. In just five seconds I was high above Rory and Clyde and zooming through the air. I was on my way with no idea of how to steer, land or stop.

CHAPTER 56

"Aaahhh!" I screamed. Below me I could see Rory dancing around and waving his arms, and I know he was yelling, but Ruggy had accelerated so quickly that I was too high to hear him.

The carpet beneath me moved and wobbled as I shifted my weight. I realized that if I fell off, I would be seriously injured. Or worse.

"Oh Ruggy, please look after me," I whispered, feeling like a complete idiot. Ruggy slowed down and even flew a little more smoothly. Huh, it was listening to me. I tried again. "So Ruggy, if that's your name, I would like to go to the Inn of the Fluffy Kitten in Tylwyth Teg, please." Ruggy just kept going and I had no idea if he understood me, or if he would do what I wanted him to. I just had to trust that he was taking me in the right direction. I lay flat on my stomach, gripped hold of the fringe at the front edge, and peeked over to watch the land of Dralfynia flash by below me.

I hadn't had time to appreciate the kingdom until now. Well, we had been pretty busy with all the kidnapping and adventures—and having to deal with the fact we were each in some kind of disturbing fairy tale of our own—so that was understandable.

Dralfynia was actually very pretty. In fact, it was beautiful. It was a sunny day, and we must have arrived in early autumn, just as it was back home, because it wasn't too hot and the fields were being harvested. The city of Timaru was lovely from the air: all pretty pink or red tiled roofs or yellow thatch with cobbled streets that looked like liquid silver from up high.

It wasn't long before we were skirting the sides of the mountain where the goblins lived, and when I sat up, I realized I could see how far Scary Forest stretched. It covered the foothills of the mountain and reached back across miles and miles of land. It was a dark stain spilling over the country. I strained my eyes trying to see the gingerbread cottage, but we weren't near enough to the center. Then I shifted my attention to see if I could spot Russell, or any of the other moving talking trees. In my curiosity, I loosed my grip; leaning too far over shifted Ruggy's balance and he tilted to the side. Before I had time to realize what was happening, I was plummeting through the sky, right down toward the cruel spiked branches that reached up out of Scary Forest. My arms and legs scrabbled in thin air, trying to get a grip of Ruggy's fringed edge again.

When the forest was so close I could smell the pine sap, Ruggy realized what had happened and zoomed beneath me so that I landed with a hefty plop in the center.

Obviously, I hadn't got the same bond with this carpet as Rory did; I guessed he hadn't forgiven me for being rude about him when we first met and I sensed that he found me annoying. Well, I had had my fright and felt bad that he needed to teach me a lesson. I told Ruggy, "Thanks," and he gave a pleased little wriggle.

Ruggy skimmed the shore of Lake Pleasant, so vast it must have covered a third of Dralfynia. It sparkled in the sunlight and was dotted with little brown rowboats, and larger craft with billowing white sails that matched the puffy clouds above. It became quite peaceful to be floating alongside the birds. Well, at least the journey was giving me some time to think. Not necessarily a good thing.

Firstly, I thought about Olive. She was a typical rich girl or so I had believed. Top in all the subjects and super pretty—she had everything I didn't. But it seemed like I had what she wanted—which was friends. I couldn't quite believe it, but I was realizing that she was jealous of me. And if I was being honest, I was a bit jealous of her, too. That didn't mean she hadn't been a bit of a bully to me and some of the other girls at school—and it didn't mean she wasn't a show-off—but it did explain why she acted the way she did. And it did make me feel bad for not trying a bit harder to be nice to her while we were all trapped in Dralfynia. Or at school, come to think of it.

Then, because I had thought about us all being trapped here, I started to think about Bridget. Hmm. I was still very uncertain about this woman. She was a stepmother after all, and you know what fairy tales say about them? That they're wicked, that's what. She had turned out to be a witch who came from a different realm—and I wasn't sure exactly why she had married my dad and taken on Rory and me. According to Aidan, she was supposed to be in Melas to look for some missing princess. Was she going to leave us if she found her? In my heart, I knew that Uncle Don had been right all along, and I would be keeping a close eye on her when we all got back home again. I wondered if I should tell Dad all about it. I pictured the conversation in my head.

"So Dad, sorry we're late for dinner, but we followed your new wife through a portal to a place called Dralfynia where we found out that she's a witch. Then we ate a gingerbread cottage, got kidnapped by goblins, went on a flying carpet, and got kidnapped again by the soldiers belonging to the Beast with Nine Fingers, who is an enemy of your new wife. Then we had to all cast a spell and we came back here. Oh yes, and I think that Olive Ayres' dad is going to develop Clyde's field into a sewage works."

Yeah, it was probably better to say nothing about all this, and just keep watching and waiting.

CHAPTER 57

We were soon over Tylwyth Teg, which looked familiar to me even from above. The little thatched houses were low and squat, the streets were made of packed earth. It was clearly poorer than Timaru, but as we swooped lower and lower, I could hear people calling to each other and laughing.

Ruggy zigzagged down and landed gently near the stables where Clyde had spent the night. I rolled him up, and hid him out of sight under a pile of fragrant hay. I closed my eyes and inhaled deeply. It smelled wonderful, but I had no time to waste. I walked out of the stable and looked all around me. There was no one around, so I hurried to the entrance of the Inn of the Fluffy Kitten and pushed the door ajar. I stood still for a couple of minutes to let my eyes adjust to the dimness inside. There were a couple of dwarves, and some humans, but no goblins. I pushed the door wider and entered the room.

Aidan was walking from table to table, wiping each one with a damp rag. The place had already started to become messy after Olive's hard work just a couple of days before.

I waited for him to notice me, and took the opportunity to watch him. I thought that I might be having my first crush on a boy and, of course, there was no way we could even be friends because he lived in Dralfynia and I lived in Melas, USA. But he was so nice—and those dimples!

It was taking an annoyingly long time for him to notice me. "Ahem," I said. He looked up, saw me, and smiled.

My heart went pitter-pat in excitement. I smiled broadly back.

Then his expression changed to horror. I whirled around. Was someone behind me? Someone like a goblin or a witch? There was nothing there. I turned back to him, puzzled and not just a little hurt.

"What?" he gasped out. "What happened to your beautiful hair?" I put my hand up to my head. Although it had started to grow again, it was still different lengths and some of the scars showed through.

"It's a long story," I said.

He came over, took me by the elbow, and led me to a quiet table.

"What happened to you?" he asked. "One minute you were here, and the next you were gone. You left your axe behind—and Clyde was still locked in our stable. I let him out, fed him, and he went off along the road to Timaru."

"Yeah, I know. I saw him there. Listen, it wasn't us being rude or anything. We got kidnapped." I told Aidan what had happened since we last met and that we needed to get hold of certain objects in order to get home. He took it all surprisingly calmly. If I hadn't experienced it myself, I would have thought that someone telling a tale like that was crazy.

"So you just came here to get one of our blankets then?" I thought he looked disappointed that I wasn't there for another reason.

I nodded, then, feeling completely reckless I said, "And to see you again, of course." My mouth went all dry, and my hands felt shaky.

He smiled at me. "I'm glad," he said. "I had hoped we could be friends." He glanced away and looked at me again.

"I saved your axe for you. I wondered if someone would come and get it. It's in the wood pile by the stable."

"I'd like to be friends, too, although I don't suppose I'll ever see you again," I replied. Aidan tilted his head to one side.

"Why?"

"Why? Well, because you live here and I live in a completely different land. I'll go home and never come back to Dralfynia again."

Aidan puffed out his cheeks and slowly blew a long breath from between his lips. "That would be a shame," he said, "but it's probably better for you; this place is full of danger."

"You're not kidding" I said, thinking of the witches, goblins, and soldiers we had met. He frowned, I had misunderstood him.

"What do you mean?" I prompted him.

"It's the prince. The one called the Beast with Nine Fingers? He has been searching for the magic flying carpet for years. And he'll do anything to get it. And what's more, he's staying here."

CHAPTER 58

Oh. That wasn't good. I needed to grab a blanket and get out of Tylwyth Teg as fast as I could. I stood up, intending to hurry upstairs to one of the bedrooms. Aidan put his hand on my shoulder and gently pressed me down again.

"He's taken a room upstairs, and his solders are in the other three rooms," he explained. Eek.

"Come with me," he said, standing up. "The king and queen are on their way over from the Isle of Merthyr to visit with their son and they'll be bringing some more blankets my parents have ordered. We can meet them on the shore of Lake Pleasant and ask for one."

I thought back to what Aidan had told me.

"So they're the parents of ..." I pointed up to the ceiling over my head where the prince was resting up with his soldiers.

"Well, yes but we'll be okay. He doesn't usually go to the lake shore to meet them. I He'll just wait for them to come here, to him." Although I wasn't happy with the 'usually' part, I didn't have a lot of options.

"All right," I said. "Let's go. But we need to be careful." As we hurried out into the sunshine, the boards above our heads creaked as someone in one of the bedrooms moved around.

The prince paced from one end of the small bedchamber to the other. The peasant innkeepers had done their best to make it comfortable, but it was far from what he was used to. These ridiculous thatched roofs encouraged rats and damp. He stretched out his hands and cracked his knuckles. There were still ten knuckles; it was only the top part of one of his fingers that had been sliced off by his sister. He needed to keep his hands nimble. His hobby meant he needed agile fingers. He glanced toward the window. It was still light, and his parents should have arrived by now. Perhaps he should stroll down to the lake side to greet them. It wouldn't do any harm to appear as if he cared. Yes, that was an excellent idea. He needed them on board to get their permission take over from that ridiculous duchess they had appointed. He would leave his bodyguards here. There was nothing to fear in this ridiculous little town. Pleased that he had something to do to break up the boredom, the prince crossed the room. He flung the door open and headed down the inn's stairs.

Aidan closed the door of the inn's main room behind him, and we hurried through the narrow streets. I had learned last time to be careful where I stepped. Carts drawn by oxen leave a certain by-product behind them. Tylwyth Teg was small, but it still took us almost half an hour to reach the shoreline because I was so fussy about where I stepped compared to the locals. I spotted a wooden jetty but it wasn't the one where the goblins had taken us. That one was a lot farther along the shore and was nothing more than some rotting planks of wood. This one was much longer and had several boats tied to it. One was a wooden rowboat, painted in a chaotic clash of bright colors. In the boat were piles of neatly folded dark gray, fluffy blankets. A woman with white hair and kind brown eyes sat in the boat, passing the blankets up to a man, who had just finished securing the boat. He was balding, with a ring of gray hair, and a gray and white beard. They were both dressed in clothes similar to those worn by Aidan and his family. I had expected a retired king and queen to have servants and wear wonderful robes and gold chains. At least a crown. Even I had a little crown! But Hazel and Michael had embraced the simple life.

We watched as Michael leaned down and helped his wife out of the boat; then the couple placed all the blankets into a little trolley that they pulled along together. They were so cute, I couldn't help but smile.

"My dear," said Hazel as she looked upward to the shore beyond the jetty. "How lovely to see you. I didn't know you were coming to meet us."

How did she know me, I wondered? I was wrong – she wasn't talking to me.

"Mother," said a man's deep voice from behind us.

CHAPTER 59

I had read books that describe terror as being like an icy finger that trails up your spine, or that it makes your knees and legs turn to jelly, or that it causes you to become rooted to the ground and unable to move.

Now that I was experiencing true terror, I can report all that those things do actually happen. The Beast with Nine Fingers was standing right behind me, and I had nowhere to run. Unless I jumped straight into the lake, I was trapped; and I didn't think I would be able to swim in my silly pink dress.

In fact, it was my terror that saved me. I hung my head low, and didn't move or speak. The prince barely noticed us. With Aidan blocking his view of me, he thought we were just a couple of ragged children.

"Leave that cart there," he instructed his parents. "Those two will take it to the inn for you." He didn't even ask us if that was okay. He just ordered us around. Aidan recovered before me.

"Yes, Your Highness," he muttered and shoved me along, keeping his own body between me and the royal party. As they walked by us, Michael and Hazel were far more polite, and both thanked us.

Hazel paused as she drew level with me, and looked at me, curiosity in her eyes.

"Have we met ...?" she began to ask.

"Mother!" the prince bellowed. He had already turned and began to outpace his parents.

She broke eye contact with me and hurried to keep up with her husband and son. I shuffled along the wooden planks of the jetty to help Aidan with the trolley, keeping my head down and repeating "I am invisible" to myself as I went. The prince was walking at such a speed that they were out of sight in a couple of minutes, and I could breathe again.

"Phew, that was close," I said.

"Yep," Aidan agreed. "The quicker we get you and these blankets back to the inn, the less chance there is of anyone recognizing you." The trolley was made of wood and was a bit like a handcart. The wooden arm that came out of one end had a t-shaped handle, so we each took one side of the handle and pulled the trolley behind us as we made our way back to the inn. Now we knew the prince and, presumably, his men were back at the inn, we could hurry without worrying about anyone spotting us.

The cart was heavy, and the wheels were wonky. It was like the worst ever supermarket trolley, and we kept having to stop and kick the wheels back so that they would run straight. It was hard work. My arms ached and we began to sweat. After almost an hour, we were back in the stable yard, and I was pulling the top blanket off to take with me.

"Do you think I should leave a note explaining that I've taken one and apologizing for not being able to pay?" I asked, feeling guilty about what I was doing.

Aidan shook his head.

"Why not?"

"Well, you don't want anyone to know you were even here, do you? And besides, we don't have any quills, or ink, or paper at the inn."

I wondered if Aidan could even read or write. I had taken it for granted that everyone could, but perhaps that wasn't the case in Dralfynia. For a minute, I felt grateful that I could go to school—and that it was all free for everyone to attend. But it was just for a minute, and I quickly got over it.

"Besides," Aidan continued. "I'm pretty sure the king and queen would let you have whatever you wanted."

"Oh that's so sweet," I remarked. "They did seem like lovely people."

Aidan took hold of the cart again. "Look, Sabrina Summers, I had better get these to my parents. We have to say goodbye now. It's too dangerous to us both for me to stay here with you." I nodded. My throat felt a little bit too tight and sore to trust with speech.

"Goodbye. Be safe," he said.

"You too," I whispered. Then, impulsively, I give him a clumsy hug. The folded blanket got in our way, and we both laughed for no real reason, feeling embarrassed.

Then Aidan turned to walk toward the inn's main door, and I turned back to the stable.

CHAPTER 60

The interior of the stable was gloomy, but I knew exactly where I had hidden Ruggy. I scuffed my way through the straw scattered on the floor to the heap of hay in the corner. Then I stopped dead in my tracks. Sitting on top of the heap of hay was the biggest, brownest, beadiest-eyed, sharpest-toothed, longest-tailed rat in the entire universe—and in the entire universe's entire history of rats.

The rat looked at me. I looked at the rat.

Rats, if you remember, are my biggest fear. I knew that all I had to do was say "shoo" and he would run away. But what if he ran toward me? Over my foot? Up my dress to my arms and face and hair? I tried to be logical. I mean, why would a rat do that? From what I had heard about rats, he was probably more afraid of me than I was of him. Although he didn't look very afraid.

I told myself that if I said "shoo," the rat would surely run straight out into the yard. My friends and brother were depending on me, and I needed to get home; I absolutely had to overcome my fear.

"Shoo!" I squeaked, making less noise than the rat himself would have done.

"Can I help you with something?" said the rat. I was so stunned that my knees folded and I sat down on the ground, hard.

"Oh dear, are you okay?" the rat asked, jumping from the hay and running toward me. I screamed long and loud.

"Oh jeez, you're quite the drama queen, aren't you?" huffed the rat, as he dodged past me into the yard.

Although I was shaking from my silly little crown to my sneakers, which were now stained with the by-products of oxen, I was sensible enough to remember that I didn't have a lot of time. A scream like that would have told half of Tylwyth Teg that I was around, so I crawled on my hands and knees and pulled Ruggy out from his hiding place. He had bits of straw and hay stuck to him, but he seemed okay. He gave a little wriggle of recognition as I took him in my arms, and I even felt a warm flutter of affection for him.

"Come on, Ruggy," I told him. "Let's get back to the others." I dragged him out to the sunshine and unrolled him, and then I hurried back into the stable to get the blanket. When I came back out, I yanked Persis' axe from the woodpile and, clutching it and the blanket in one hand, I threw myself flat onto the carpet and called out:

"Up, up and away!"

"Oh no, my dear, I don't think so," said the voice I had heard down at the jetty. A shiny black boot thumped down onto Ruggy, right by my left hand; meanwhile, Ruggy was starting to move and buck in an attempt to take off. I squeezed my eyes closed in a crazy 'if I can't see the bad guy, he can't see me' kind of way and I released my grip of the axe and the blanket. I pushed at the boot with my left hand as my right gripped hard onto Ruggy's fringe. I didn't want to fall off if he took off suddenly.

Success! The boot lifted and Ruggy rose an inch into the air. But then the boot dropped again, smashing against my fingers. I screamed as the boot rose again, no doubt with the intention of trying to crush my hand again. Ruggy came to the rescue. Dear, wonderful, Ruggy who I had always liked, right from the get go. He took full advantage of that fraction of a second to take off vertically, leaving my stomach behind—and, luckily, the prince and his vicious feet.

"Yikes!" I shrieked and opened my eyes. Level with my eyes, a hand shot up and gripped Ruggy's fringe: a hand with only three fingers and a thumb. Ruggy was pulled down, and shook himself from side to side, trying to free himself. I swung wildly around, holding on as tight as I could.

"No!" I shrieked, and did the only thing I could think of. I stretched out my fingers and closed them around the smooth wooden handle of the axe. I had to yank the blade free from where it was tangled in Ruggy's fringe then I lifted it up and let it drop on the prince's hand, sharp edge down. I had only meant to scare him, not to do any real damage, but I heard him howl with pain and he released his grip. I dragged the axe back toward me and stared in horror at the blade. It was stained with red, and had most of a man's middle finger stuck to it. I shrieked, panicked and waved the axe around until the finger flew off and fell to the earth.

That was all Ruggy needed. Freed, he shot upward and the precious blanket started to slip off behind me. Holding on by my fingertips, I managed to stretch back and snag it just as it began to fall. As I pulled myself into the center of Ruggy, I risked looking down. I saw the figure of the prince below me. He was curled into a ball on the ground, nursing his injured hand. They would have to call him the Beast with Eight Fingers now.

Good.

CHAPTER 61

Finally!

Finally we were on our way home. On our return journey, Ruggy flew as fast as he could, directly to Timaru—no scenic route this time. As he circled around during his descent, I saw below us a patch of green grass. As Ruggy dipped lower, I could make out Olive, Rory, Persis and Clyde all watching me. When she spotted me and saw me flap the blanket in the air like a victory flag, Persis began to gesture and waved toward a pile of logs, looking upset. I raised her axe above my head and waved it at her. As soon as she spotted it, she began to twirl around and did a crazy dance of joy, which seemed a bit over the top to me, but when I landed I understood why.

Persis took the axe from me and explained that she hadn't been able to find any other axes to chop a log into smaller pieces of kindling. Without it, she hadn't been able to start the fire. She dragged out a fat log, laid it down on its flat, cut side and lifted the axe above her head. With a mighty swing, she brought it down and the log splintered into sticks. She scooped them up and carefully placed them at the base of the fire. I guess being a Girl Scout teaches you some useful stuff. As Persis was doing something very complicated with stones and dry grass to make a spark, she finally noticed the dark stain on the blade.

"It's a long story," I said.

"When we get home, I'll tell you guys all about it." I rolled Ruggy up and dragged him and the blanket across the grass to the others. Before we cast the spell, there was something I knew I had to do—and I had to do it fast before I lost my nerve.

I stood up and faced Olive.

"I'm sorry I was so mean to you," I said very quickly.

Three faces were amazed; three mouths dropped open.

"Uh, thanks Sabrina," Olive spluttered out. "I'm sorry, too. I was never nice to you at school." She tugged at her skirt, and continued, "I said some pretty nasty things about your clothes, but look at me now. I should have taken more notice of the person you are, not what you wore." Then she added, in a rush of words, "And thanks for apologizing in front of everyone else."

"Yeah, no problem" I shrugged it off, although inside I was thinking, "What's wrong with my clothes? Doesn't everyone wear denim shorts every day of the year?" But I was pleased she had noticed that I had made my apology in front of Persis and Rory and Clyde. After all, what's the point of doing something noble if no one notices? I had been mean to her in front of people; the least I could do was apologize in front of them.

This felt like the right moment to hug Olive, but fortunately the fire crackled as it began to burn in earnest. It was time. Time to cast this insane spell, and to pit blind hope against cold, scientific logic by believing that it would take us all home again.

"Ready?" I asked everyone. I held the blanket, ready to throw it onto the fire.

"No," said Rory. I stared at him.

"What's up, Rory?" asked his two-girl fan club in unison. He pointed to the ground. "Ruggy; we can't leave Ruggy behind." I began to argue with him.

"Don't be silly," I said. "He'll be much happier here. If we take him home, he'll just live on the floor and won't have other magic carpets to play with." It was a good point, but one that Olive completely ruined by dropping a bombshell on us.

"Actually ..." she said, "actually, we probably should take Ruggy with us, you know, to keep him safe from the prince and everything.

And then maybe someone can collect Ruggy and take him back, when the other two magic objects have been found and when the true ruler of Dralfynia is able to take over from Duchess Yvonne."

I had vaguely remembered all that stuff about the politics and rulers from Aidan, but hadn't taken as much notice of it as she had. But I did remember the prince trying to wrench Ruggy from under me, and I realized she was right. I wasn't sure why I should care about any other magic objects, though. I mean, Dralfynia was full of them.

"Which other objects?" I demanded.

"The glass slipper and the magic slingshot," chanted Persis and Rory together.

Oh yes ... them. But what did any of this have to do with us? We were never, ever coming back to Dralfynia again. We were going to our old lives and putting all this behind us. Weren't we? I thought about what they had said, but there was something wrong with their logic.

"If we take Ruggy back to Melas, how would he get back to Dralfynia when someone needed him? I mean, none of us would have the first idea of how to travel back again, would we? I don't think this spell would work again." Olive had obviously been thinking about this though, and had an answer.

"Your stepmother," she replied.

I was shaking my head before she had even finished speaking.

"No way," I said. "I can't tell her we followed her here, and that we know her secret. Rory and I would be grounded for the rest of our lives."

Olive shifted her weight from foot to foot, trying to come up with a solution. "Well, we'll have to find somewhere to hide him then, and somehow get a message to this duchess woman, or to Aidan."

We stood, watching the flames leap from stick to stick, desperately trying to think of a fast answer to our problem.

In the end, it was blind panic that took Ruggy from Dralfynia to Melas, rather than any well thought out, sensible plan.

CHAPTER 62

"Hey, you kids! What are you doing lighting fires in the middle of Timaru? Don't you know it's dangerous?" a gruff voice yelled at us from the far side of the grassy square where we stood.

Well, I suppose we were being a bit optimistic in thinking we could light a fire in broad daylight and not have a grown-up come and yell at us.

"Quick, quick," I cried. "Let's do the spell." I gripped Ruggy with one arm, and watched as Olive threw her sticky wooden spoon onto the fire. Whatever the brown stuff was, it was highly flammable and the flames shot higher. Next it was Rory. Concentrating hard, he edged as close to the heat as he dared and, leaning over, he opened his bunched fist and a single long hair from Clyde's tail floated down. It caught a gust of hot air and whirled up high for a few seconds, before floating gently down to the fire and sizzling instantly into tiny orange sparks. Now it was my turn. With my free arm, I threw the blanket onto the fire.

Oh dear. In Melas, we have fire blankets in our school. They are supposed to be thrown onto fires because they stop the oxygen from feeding it. They smother the flames. Apparently the same law of science applied here because that's exactly what my cat fur blanket did right then. As we watched in horror, the fire began to die out. And to make matters worse, a group of half a dozen citizens of Timaru were shouting at us and heading our way. Then, one tiny flame broke through the dark gray of the blanket and, with a terrific "whoosh", the entire thing began to blaze—and the little fire became an inferno.

That really got the Timaruvians going.

Clyde rested his great head on top of mine, and I grabbed Olive's hand, still clutching Ruggy with my other arm. She took Persis by the hand and Persis reached out to Rory's hand. Unfortunately Rory didn't want to hold hands—he was a big boy now. He shook her off and folded his arms stubbornly.

"Rory, you doofus. Take Persis' hand so you can look after her. She's a bit scared," I called across.

Persis glared at me.

Rory did as he was told and we chanted very, very quickly.

"Back to my home and back to my time; back to my home and back to my time; back to my home and back to my time."

We closed our eyes. Rory counted.

"One. Two. Three."

Nothing. I opened one of my eyes and peeked out. The citizens were at the well, hauling up big wooden buckets of water and looking our way. They were going to put out the fire. But, before I could start to beg them to leave it alone, I saw a sudden puff of purple, sparkling smoke, and smelled boiled cabbage. The stomach-churning roller coaster that we had been on just a few days earlier began again.

Up and down, around and around, hot and cold. At one point, I think my feet were where my head should have been and my skin felt raw where the magic smoke scraped across it. Then there was a thump, followed by blissful peace and darkness.

But not for long. I lay on the grass with my eyes closed, listening to the sounds around me. I was frightened, I admit it. What if I opened my eyes and saw the faces of angry Timaruvians instead of sky above the field opposite my house? Then I heard a comforting sound and knew I was home.

Clyde farted. He had gone straight to the apple tree in his field and had started to feast. Then there was another sound: the noise of Olive dry retching. After that came a sensation: a thumping against my hip.

Rory was gently, but annoyingly, kicking me to get me moving. I put my hand down to shove his foot away and felt denim.

Denim! I was wearing denim cut-offs, not that terrible dress. It was the happiest I had felt in ages. I sat up. I touched my head. No spiky crown—and normal hair all over my head.

"Guys, takeout pizza on me, from my allowance," I said.

CHAPTER 63

Two hours later, we were in my room, licking grease from our fingers and burping happily. Persis and Olive had gotten permission from their parents to stay with me for dinner, and Clyde had gone back to being an ordinary Clydesdale horse in his field. Rory had laid Ruggy out on his bedroom floor. He had tried to get him to fly, but it seemed that Ruggy was tired. So Rory sat cross-legged in the middle of Ruggy and drew sketches of the friend he missed the most: Russell.

I lay back on my bed and yawned. Having strange adventures really takes it out of you. Still, it was all over now. I let my eyelids droop and began to doze. I was aware of the others still talking. I heard Olive saying something about talking to her dad about not building a sewage works in Clyde's field. That would be nice of her, if she could persuade him not to do it. We'd probably never really like each other, but at least we could tolerate one another now.

Just as long as Persis stayed my best friend and Olive kept away from Aidan, that is. I turned on my side and buried my head deeper into my pillows and let my mind drift to Aidan. It wasn't just the dimples that made me like him, it was the way he helped us. He didn't treat us like outsiders, and he had no idea about bullying. He was so uncomplicated. But then, life in Dralfynia seemed very uncomplicated altogether. People were either good guys or bad guys. No one had judged us on how we looked, or the clothes we wore, or how great we were at sport or math. As I drifted off to sleep, I heard Dad coming home and calling out that he was back. My last thought was that I hoped Rory hadn't eaten the pizza I had saved for Dad.

When I woke up the next morning, the first thing I did was check my appearance in the mirror—a mirror that didn't talk back to me like the one Olive had told us about but one that did nothing more than reflect my sleep-crumpled face and sticking-out hair.

Maybe it was all a dream, I thought. Maybe Dralfynia didn't exist, and Bridget was just a normal person?

No such luck. As I drifted past Rory's room on my way to the bathroom, I saw Ruggy on his floor. It was all real—but at least it was all over.

Except for Bridget.

When I reached the kitchen, she was there making blueberry pancakes. I had thought that only TV and movie families had pancakes for breakfast, but she wasn't doing too bad a job. She turned and smiled at me, a dripping wooden spoon in her hand. I checked it out. It wasn't charred from being thrown into a magical fire, it was just a normal wooden spoon covered in pancake batter.

Well, I guess I had gotten away with it. I had discovered her secret and I would be keeping a close eye on her from now on—and she knew nothing about it. I smiled right back at her as I took the plate of pancakes and jug of maple syrup that she offered me.

I walked to school that day. I'd done so much walking in Dralfynia that my fitness had improved. I was feeling pretty good about myself. It was a nice day, and I had all my mobile devices fully charged and in my backpack. I planned to sit and watch TV all evening long, at the same time as doing some online shopping and checking out my friends' latest uploaded photos on social media.

In the school hallway, as I fiddled with the padlock on my locker, Olive ran up to me. I wondered how this would go. We were back in our usual environment, so would we go back to being enemies? She grabbed hold of my arm and shook me hard. Persis appeared behind her.

"Hey, take it easy," she snapped at Olive. "It's not totally her fault." Olive glared at Persis and then at me.

"Sabrina, we have to leave school right now," Olive said.

"Why? No. No way. And anyway, why? And what's not totally my fault?" I said.

"You're going to have to tell your stepmom everything, because we need her to put all this right." Olive was insistent and she was getting on my nerves.

"But why?" I wailed. What was it with these two?

"Because of the new teacher," Persis told me. "We have a new Home Room and cookery teacher." As she spoke, I felt the corridor grow chilly and had that feeling you get when you somehow know that a person is right behind you.

I turned and stared at the figure of a woman. She wore a black pants suit and had long black hair tied into a neat bun. She had a name badge with "Ms. Wu" engraved on it. She had one black eye and one green eye.

She smiled.

EPILOGUE

In Dralfynia, Cinderella woke up from a deep sleep. The fireplace that she slept beside was cold. She shook herself awake and began to sweep away the dead ashes.

That was such a strange dream, she thought to herself. I dreamed I was in another land where magic did not exist.

Not far away, deep in Scary Forest, a little girl, with a red cloak hanging from a peg on her bedroom door, jumped from her bed and ran to her father's knee. He sat at the table, sharpening his axe.

"Daddy," she said, "Daddy, I had a funny dream last night."

"Did you sweetheart? Tell me all about it," he smiled.

Much, much further away, a boy—who was supposed to be selling precious oil from a stone jar that was as tall as him—was shaken from a dream by his uncle.

"Sleeping on the job? We have a customer, Ali. Wake up lad," he said. Ali Baba rubbed his eyes.

"Uncle, I had such a funny dream," Ali said sleepily, "but now I can't remember it."

And in a tall tower at the edge of the kingdom, Rapunzel sat up, stretched her arms, and yawned. She touched the top of her head.

"Oh thank goodness; I dreamed that my crown had gone," she said.

ABOUT THE AUTHOR

Michele Clark McConnochie has worked in education as a teacher and manager for over 20 years. These days, she is also a freelance writer and creative writing teacher who lives in Christchurch, New Zealand with her husband Brent, his daughter Steph, and their two very spoilt rescue cats, Twinkle and Cleo. She supports Wolverhampton Wanderers Football Club and likes Dr. Who, Snoopy, chocolate and reading. Her favorite book when she was young was 'Little Women.'

One of Michele's passions is making the joy of reading and stories available to all readers, and that is why Morgan James Kids has made this book as easy to read as possible. Michele also sells dyslexia-friendly versions of her books through her website or via Amazon.com.

Did you know that animal rescue centers around the world have heaps of animals who desperately need a place to live? If you are looking for a pet and can provide a kind, loving home, why not check out your nearest animal shelter, just like Queen Hazel and King Michael do?

If you've enjoyed this book, why not review it? Authors love to get feedback.

And if you would like to contact Michele, she would be thrilled to hear from you. Visit www.MCMauthor.com, follow her on Facebook at facebook.com/micheleclarkmcconnochie, or follow her on Twitter @ MicheleClarkMcC.

If you want to read more about the people of Dralfynia, you can sign up to Michele's newsletter and you will get receive a free e-book, Tales from Dralfynia! Go to www.MCMauthor.com to find out more.

Author photograph courtesy of Stephanie McConnochie.

Morgan James makes all of our titles available
through the Library for All Charity Organization.

www.LibraryForAll.org